OTTO PENZLER PRESENTS
AMERICAN MYSTERY CLASSICS

THE CAT
WEARS A NOOSE

DOLORES HITCHENS (1907–1973) was a highly prolific mystery author who wrote under multiple pseudonyms and in a range of styles. A large number of her books, including the Rachel Murdock series, were published under the D. B. Olsen moniker, but she is perhaps best remembered today for her later novel, *Fool's Gold*, published under her own name, which was adapted for film as *Bande à part* by Jean-Luc Godard.

RHYS BOWEN is the *New York Times* bestselling author of two historical mystery series as well as several internationally best-selling historical novels. She was born in Bath, England, and educated at London University but now divides her time between California and Arizona. Her books have been nominated for every major mystery award and she has won twenty of them to date, including five Agathas. Her books have been translated into over thirty languages.

THE CAT
WEARS A NOOSE

DOLORES
HITCHENS

Writing as
D.B. Olsen

Introduction by
RHYS
BOWEN

AMERICAN
MYSTERY
CLASSICS

Penzler Publishers
New York

Published in 2024 by Penzler Publishers
58 Warren Street, New York, NY 10007
penzlerpublishers.com

Distributed by W. W. Norton

Cover image: Andy Ross
Cover design: Mauricio Diaz

Paperback ISBN 978-1-61316-491-4
Hardcover ISBN 978-1-61316-490-7

Library of Congress Control Number: 2023918553

Printed in the United States of America

9 8 7 6 5 4 3 2 1

THE CAT
WEARS A NOOSE

INTRODUCTION

When I was asked to write a forward to this book and I saw it was by an American author, written in 1944 I was not expecting what I read. I googled D. B Olsen and found that she was a.k.a. Dolores Hitchens and had written a lot of books from the nineteen thirties to the fifties.

I grew up reading the ladies of the Golden Age—Christie, Sayers, Tey, Allingham, Marsh. . . all British except for New Zealander Marsh. I tried reading American crime writers—Hammett, Spillane—but frankly they weren't my cup of tea. I liked my mysteries to be cozier, character-driven, tinged with humor and taking place in a world where everything would be put right by the end of the book.

So imagine my surprise when the book opened with a lyrical description of moonlight and focused on an elderly lady with knitted cape and gloves coming home through an elegant neighborhood from a meeting of the Methodist Ladies' Aid and witnessing a murder. This could have been the start of any of those books I had so enjoyed as a child. I realized that it was not England by the pepper tree in a garden and this was confirmed by learning it was actually Los Angeles. But not the Los Ange-

II · RHYS BOWEN

les we think of—the brash town of movies and freeways. It was Miss Marple's St. Mary Mead moved to America!

Here were well-heeled families, nosy neighbors and old ladies with cats. The police detective was friendly and easy going, long suffering in his relationship with the heroine, Miss Rachel—a confident amateur detective. Was Los Angeles really like this in the 1940s? Perhaps it was. Anyway, I immediately felt at home following Miss Rachel as she uses her powers of observation and her experience to outwit the police.

In many ways she is the American version of Miss Marple—she's astute, with a strong sense of justice. But she doesn't behave like Miss Marple. She takes risks Miss Marple would never have taken—placing herself in a household where a murder has just taken place, spying on people, sneaking into rooms. Miss Marple was always content to observe from the background, unnoticed. And Miss Marple would never have put a relative in jeopardy, nor would she have been so cavalier about her pets. In fact, Miss Rachel comes across as a person with that sense of justice but with not much compassion. See what you think.

The other interesting factor about the book is that it is the third in a series, all written during WWII. If the book had taken place in Britain there would have been bombing, danger, deprivation and heroism. Here one is only vaguely aware of the war because the son of the family has been wounded at Pearl Harbor and because servants now leave to work in factories for more money. Apart from the odd mention, life goes on smoothly in Parchly Heights as it has always done. The family eats duck and shops for new clothes. One member drinks too much. No, this could not have taken place in England where people were close to starving and everything was rationed!

For me it was entertaining enough to keep reading, occasionally containing some lovely lyrical passages of description. There were red herrings and suspects aplenty, clues placed throughout but it lacks the subtlety of character observation and realism of some of her British contemporaries.

—RHYS BOWEN

1

Outside the moon filled the night with such a silver flood that Miss Jennifer Murdock stood still to take it in. Beyond the black shadow of the pepper tree the garden lay distinct, transfixed, and the street and the houses facing on it were painted with a motionless light in which jutting curbs and cornices and window embrasures stood etched in darkness and in which the rest was more fantastically clear than by day.

There was no sound except the rustle of a bird high in the tree and the closing of the house door very softly behind her.

Miss Jennifer pulled her little knitted cape high about her throat, snapped the buttons of her woolen gloves, shook the petticoats under her taffeta skirt for easier walking, and began to pick her way along the flagstones to the gate. She carried under one arm the account book of the Parchly Heights Methodist Ladies' Aid and in the other hand her spectacle case. The account book had displayed a shortage of fifty-eight cents, and she and Mrs. Brenn had been until now discovering the error. Miss Jennifer's eyes stung with weariness. The effect of the moonlight and the silence was chilling and a little eerie; she wished suddenly that she had let the error go and had left earlier for home.

The grass of Mrs. Brenn's lawn shone with a silver frost, and the water in the birdbath gave back the light with the trembling brilliance of a mirror. The gate moved with a faint squeak; its crisscross of shadow touched Miss Jennifer's shoe and then swung back. There was no other person abroad upon the street. There was only the moon, the breathless light, and the stillness—and a feeling of nervous discomfort that hovered near Miss Jennifer's heart.

She had taken no more than five steps away from the gate when there came, from the other side of the silence, the rattle and thunder of a car. An old car, Miss Jennifer thought, from the noise of it and the uneven explosions of its cylinders. She was a little glad to have had the silence shattered, and she watched the far end of the street to see if the car would turn toward her.

The headlights, canary-colored eyes in the white glow cast by the moon, swung into sight some blocks away. The motor coughed on the slight rise; the high, old-fashioned chassis swayed. Then the car slowed suddenly and crept against the curb. The occupant, Miss Jennifer thought, must be searching for a number.

It came on by jerks and starts. With a long *squeech* of the brakes it pulled to a halt almost opposite. A voice, a rather blurry thick voice, said loudly: "Thanks, old man. Thanks. Can't say how I 'preciate you bringing me home."

Another voice, also masculine, but with traces of impatience, answered: "Don't mention it. Glad to help."

A figure, the figure of a big man, had clambered out the opposite door and stood, half visible to Miss Jennifer through the car windows, on the sidewalk. "I want to pay for the gas. Ought to do that. Least I can do. Right, isn't it?" And something about the tone, the slurred syllables, the uncertain timing, caused Miss Jennifer to realize that the man was drunk. The figure, through the glass, swayed a trifle as it fumbled through its clothes. "Can't seem to find m' wallet. See it inside anywhere?"

There was a brief search. "Nah. It ain't in here. Look in your pockets, bud."

"Oh. Here it is. You could use a dollar, couldn't you?"

"Nah, let it go. Look, I've got to get rolling. Can you make the steps all right or do you want me to help you?"

The man on the sidewalk stood still in a curious silence. Then he said with the heavy sarcasm of the thoroughly liquored: "Say, you aren't insinuating anything, are you? You don't happen to think I'm drunk, do you?"

"Nah, I didn't mean a thing. Forget it. Skip it."

"Because"—he leaned back into the car, a black gargoyle against the white night, finger wagging in the driver's profile—"because if I thought you meant I was drunk, I'd bring you inside and damned well drink you un'er the table. See?"

"Disgusting!" Miss Jennifer murmured, and began to walk very quickly out of earshot.

"Not drunk a bit!" persisted the man on the sidewalk.

"Sure you ain't." The old car hummed, had hiccups, slammed into noisy gear, and began to creep away. "Good night. Look out for the steps, though."

In the unreality of moonlight the scene had the silly disconnectedness of a bad farce. The staggering man, the old car, the meaningless argument, all played against the background of the two-story stucco home, were, in Miss Jennifer's opinion, poor theater. The actors just didn't belong to their surroundings: to the neat rectitude of Parchly Heights, to the prim lawns and privet hedges, the air of established wealth, the sobriety and quiet.

She tried to remember who lived in the house before which the drunken man had alighted and could not recall knowing the people there.

She had come to a corner, where Mrs. Brenn's lawn ended at a cross street; some touch of curiosity made her look back. There had been silence since the departure of the car. Through a fog of moonbeams she saw the figure of the man it had left; he was on his hands and knees crawling up the steps of the stucco house. His body looked hunched and buglike, and he was having obvious difficulties with his legs.

A habit of helpfulness made Miss Jennifer turn full around. Then she checked herself. It would, after all, not be proper for a spinster of seventy-two to go to the aid of—she stumbled mentally over the common term—of a drunk.

The man had reached the vestibule, a severely classic little entry with pillars, its door dark under an arch. He crawled to his knees and then inched upright and stood swaying with an arm about a column. After a while there was the tinkle of keys, and Miss Jennifer relaxed. Once inside, she felt, he should be among friends.

He staggered into the oval space before the door, his figure blending with the other darkness. There was the metallic click of a lock opening, the faint screech of a hinge.

And then out of utter stillness, out of the darkness at the door, came the crash of gunfire. There was a flash of blue flame, a belching roar, a thin sharp odor which stained the night.

Miss Jennifer felt shock run through her like the arrowing of a little knife. She trembled and put a hand over her lips to shut off a scream. The figure of the man had slumped, though in the dark entry she could not see just how he lay; he clawed at the door and made a whimpering sound that reached her across the moonlit space. In a dazed and incredulous moment Miss Jennifer found herself running toward him. She passed the privet hedge, and a branch of it snagged her taffeta skirt, and there was a short sound of ripping. At the entry she stumbled and put a hand briefly on a column for support.

A light came on inside the entry, a yellow beam bisected the porch and showed him lying there.

He had been a man of nearly forty, to judge from his build and his flesh and his trace of baldness. There was about him a loose, gross air, a sort of slovenliness hard to define, a hint of carelessness and dissipation. His clothes were not quite up to Parchly Heights; they were poorly assembled, poorly pressed.

He lay on one side facing the crack of light. One large flabby hand still held the bunch of keys, spattered bloodily with red, and red had crept down into his collar and shirt front and into the lapels of his brown worsted coat.

There was no way of knowing whether she had ever seen his face before. There was, on the drunken man, no longer any face. Nor did he move now or make the whimpering sound. He was quite and inevitably dead.

Miss Jennifer stood shuddering, but even in that moment she saw that there was no one in the vestibule, no crouching form, no hidden murderer. The dead man was entirely alone, save for herself. The door—she was sure of this point—had not opened beyond the small crack, far too narrow to admit a human body. No figure had run out into the moonlight from the porch.

Miss Jennifer stared about her, at the little oval alcove before the door. Two niches in the wall on either side held pottery vases. "But how—?" she whispered in the half-dark to the man at her feet.

A cool voice said on the other side of the door, "I'm going to look, John. That didn't sound just right, did it?"

There were steps, a woman's steps, approaching the crack of light. Horror and confusion urged Miss Jennifer to get away, not to be embroiled in whatever violence was due to be uncovered. She ran like a mouse off the steps and out into the moonlit street. There was the stench of gunpowder in her nose and a fixed hope in her mind that this would turn out to be a dream and that she would find herself at home in bed when she reached the next corner.

Parchly Heights—at least the part of it surrounding the house with the privet hedge—was coming gradually to life with lights, with discreet voices, with hesitant door openings and peepings forth.

Miss Jennifer found her own corner, her own quiet street, and turned there with a little sob and sank down onto the curb. "It was real," she thought. "I actually did stand there and see a man shot to death. In his own doorway—at least he had keys to the house, even if he didn't look as though he belonged in it. He was shot from inside the entry. *And there wasn't anyone else there. . . .*"

She looked at the moonlight, a limitless flood going off into infinity, and at the hill where, beyond a stretch of vacant property, stood the house she shared with her sister Rachel.

Miss Rachel by now should be yawning in the sleepy quiet of the parlor, her black cat curled up by her toes, her book closed in her lap.

Miss Rachel's book was called *The Corpse with the Cunning Eye*, and if there was one thing that she loved meddling with, to the frustration of Lieutenant Stephen Mayhew and the incredulous horror of Miss Jennifer, it was murder.

Sitting on the curb, shivering and sick, Miss Jennifer made a great resolve: that nothing short of death itself could make her reveal to Rachel the part she had played in that night's terror. For if she were to know, of course Miss Rachel would be in the middle of things at once.

Miss Rachel was startled awake by some slight noise. She looked first at her book; *The Corpse with the Cunning Eye* had dropped from her lap to the floor. She bent to pick it up and then stayed that way, half crouched over, her nose only a few inches from the inquiring one of the cat. The gas sputtered a little, and the ticking of the clock on the mantel was loud in the drowsy room.

She had heard again the noise that had wakened her, the sound of a quiet step in the hall beyond the living-room door.

"It's Jennifer," she thought, and then: "No, it isn't. Jennifer puffs when she comes in, and Mrs. Brenn always irritates her so that she bangs the account book down on the hall table before she takes off her wraps. Whoever this is, he's being very quiet. I wonder if we're really at last going to have burglars?"

Someone rapped very softly on the doorjamb.

"Is anyone inside?" It was a young voice, a girl's voice. "Is anyone at home?"

Miss Rachel breathed again and straightened in her chair. "Come in," she said.

A girl in a dark blue coat and wearing a blue veil tied over her hair and under her chin came into sight in the doorway. She was slight and small of figure; her face was thin, and there was a smudge of tiredness under each eye. She tried to smile at Miss Rachel, but her lips trembled in doing it and she bit at them and seemed at a loss for words.

Miss Rachel indicated a needle-point-covered chair to the right of her own. "Won't you sit down?"

The girl gave her an uncertain glance. "I—I must apologize first for coming in as I did. I rapped at your door, you see, and no one came and I—" She stopped and seemed to take a deep breath. "I was afraid to stay outdoors and I slipped inside. Your front door wasn't fastened."

"Have you fastened it now?"

"Yes." She came a few steps into the room. "That was all right, wasn't it?"

"It was perfectly all right." Miss Rachel put her book upon a stand and plumped the little pillow at her back. She looked more pleased than anything. Her small face under its puff of white hair, always pleasant, beamed at the hesitant girl in the door. "Come in and tell me about it."

The girl walked with a curious softness, a sort of subservience, as though she were trying to blend with the furnishings and be invisible. She slid upon the chair and after a moment she untied the veil and let it fall back upon her shoulders. She had thick hair, quite dark. It somehow made her look thinner and paler than before.

"I must apologize for coming here as I have, late at night, without any appointment."

Something in the latter phrase caught Miss Rachel's notice. "What makes you think I make appointments?"

The girl looked at her confidently. "You are a detective, aren't you?"

There was only an instant during which Miss Rachel showed any surprise. Then a pink spot came into each of her cheeks and a businesslike air seemed to settle over her. "I have handled a few things in my time," she said casually. "Suppose you begin now at the beginning and tell me what's frightened you."

The girl took the veil and wadded it nervously into her fingers and then let it dangle before the cat. "There isn't really a beginning. It always was there, in my uncle's house, from the day I first came into it. A feeling. A feeling as though someone hated me, hated me so much that—" She stopped, made a helpless mute gesture with the hand holding the veil.

"Feelings are based on concrete evidence, whether we realize it or not," Miss Rachel told her. "There must have been something, some small incident, that caused you to believe what you do."

"Little things were always going wrong," the girl said. "Ink would be spilled in a room I had just dusted; dishes be broken and half hidden in the trash box; wilted flowers put out when there were guests. But until tonight—" She stopped, and Miss Rachel saw that she was shaking, that some inner grief was clawing at her, and that she was fighting for self-control. "Tonight my little bird died." She had put a hand into the pocket of her coat and was removing a small bundle wrapped in a man's cotton handkerchief. "He had convulsions. He must have suffered terribly. Pete helped me give him water, but it didn't do any good."

The handkerchief fell open to reveal a wad of crumpled yellow feathers, two spidery feet stiffened in death, a beak from which no more song would flow.

The girl turned away to weep, and Miss Rachel took the bird and bent with it toward the light.

2

THE GIRL's visit marked, in Miss Rachel's mind, the beginning of the affair she decided eventually to call the Case of the Sliver of Doubt, in which she played a game of wits with Murder over such trivialities as a cologne bottle, a red robe, a wedding ring in a nest of cotton, a werewolf, and a woman who wore garlic.

If there had been a sliver of doubt as to whom the most valid of these clues had led, there would be, in Miss Rachel's mind, quite a different state of affairs in the house on Chestnut Street. The red robe with its secret would be hanging in the last recesses of the closet of a young woman who would have had no further use for it—being in prison or worse. The wedding ring would have been buried, deeply and darkly, with its original owner. The cologne bottle would have been full again of fragrance. And the woman who wore garlic and was afraid of the thing on the wall should have found a happier job.

These things, though mute, were eloquent under Miss Rachel's inquiring mind. She had no difficulty over them.

As to the werewolf, Miss Rachel prefers not to think. There are deeps in the human soul like the chasm in the western Pacific, where strange things swim, where old terrors peer from their medieval darkness, where long shapes coil and seem asleep, where the unbelieved comes to life. She burned the werewolf, and it returned from ashes to haunt her; and there are moments yet when she dreams that she stands in the black hall of the house on Chestnut Street and sees the wolf-like shape crouch in the eye of a green glow and feels old and unnamed terrors grip her.

Not that the case depended on the dark for any of its chills. There were moments in daylight, in the warm commonplaceness of morning and afternoon: moments like the one when she saw Mrs. Terrice's ghost, grown old, fade from the rear of the garage; moments like the one she spent under a bed watching a man's feet circle her; moments like the one in her own living room, where her cat growled faintly and a murderer's footfall was soft in the still air. Or the moment she stood in a bathroom door and felt time dissolve and saw the horror some believed in long ago come to life: the long prints on the tile and the limp thing they had circled with its blood.

It was for a time complicated, terrifying, sickeningly baffling, but out of it Miss Rachel got part of a bride's bouquet, a great Dane, and the experience of being a cook. And Miss Jennifer obtained her great adventure. Which Miss Rachel considers sufficient reward for anybody.

She turned the rumpled ball of feathers over and stroked it gently with a forefinger.

"How old are you, my dear?"

The girl dried her eyes fiercely with the back of a hand. "Eighteen. Nineteen next month."

"And your name?"

"Shirley Melissa Grant."

"Your parents?"

"Dead."

"You spoke about living in your uncle's house," Miss Rachel said gently. "Tell me about that: how you came to be there, how long, and so on."

"My uncle is Mr. John Terrice. He lives at 1350 Chestnut Street. It's a nice house, a lovely home, just as they promised me it would be."

"Promised you?"

"When Mother died. Mother, you see, had wanted me to go to live with Grandmother Grant in Michigan. She is my father's mother, very elderly but nice. Mother thought, for some reason she didn't explain, that I would be happier there. But Uncle John persuaded me after the funeral that I should come to live with them here in Los Angeles. Only he called it Hollywood, and it sounded exciting."

"Parts of what people call Hollywood can be very dull," Miss Rachel said. "And it's true he misled you in giving it that name. This is strictly Los Angeles. It's Parchly Heights. We aren't even Beverly Hills."

The girl looked at the bundle of yellow feathers and her lips shook. "I've been with my uncle and his family a little more than a year. It—it hasn't been dull. At first it was strange, and lately it's been terrifying. Sometimes I'm afraid that I'm imagining things, slowly but surely going crazy. Young people can go crazy, can't they?"

"I wouldn't worry too much over that possibility," Miss Rachel counseled. "Just when did you first get this feeling that someone in the house hated you very greatly?"

"I don't know." A drear, peaked look had come into her face. "It just came over me gradually. A lot of little accidents happened. I was blamed for them. I began to keep watch. I found things ready to happen: a vase on the very edge of the mantel where even so much as a step might jar it off, a broom poked through a window light and covered with a curtain—but not covered so well my aunt wouldn't notice it." She suddenly put a hand miserably over her eyes. "They were just tiny, hateful things, not really hurting anybody. Not even, perhaps, meant to get me into trouble. Just mischief, maybe, the way a bad little boy might do. Until tonight. Until my little bird died."

"The house sounds as though it were bewitched," Miss Rachel mused, staring at the ruffled feathers. "And these accidents, as you call them, have an odd sound. You were—" She hesitated, as if seeking a tactful word. "You were, after a fashion, rather a housemaid in your uncle's house, weren't you?"

"I am," the girl said, bringing it into the present. "That was another thing that came over me gradually. A maid quit, and they talked about the labor shortage and all made shift to do the work between them. Only in the end I seemed to be doing it all."

"I see." Miss Rachel wrapped the bird gently back into the man's handkerchief and rose and took it with her to a tiny desk, where she sat down and took from a drawer a sheet of paper and a pen.

"I would like for you to give me now the names of everyone in your uncle's household," she said to the girl, who sat broody and tearful, stroking the cat. "And their ages, too, perhaps. And how they've acted toward you."

The girl straightened uncomfortably in the chair. "I was wondering, Miss Murdock, about your fee. I know you're quite famous—I've read about you in the papers—and perhaps what you charge would be more than I could pay. I can't let you go ahead until I explain that."

"We won't worry about a fee," Miss Rachel said, "until we see where all this leads us. There may not even be any."

The girl relaxed, found a handkerchief in her coat pocket and blew her nose into it, and said, "You're about the nicest person I've met out here. I guess you must be a lot like my Grandmother Grant."

"Thank you. And now your uncle's family, please."

"Well . . ." The girl puckered her dark eyebrows in a little frown. "There's my uncle. I suppose we'd better begin with him. His name is John Terrice, as I told you, and I guess he's about fifty. He was very nice to me when I first came, and then the niceness sort of wore away, and he treats me now like a—a servant. Which I am, I guess. He just doesn't speak except to ask me to clean the ash trays or to please bring him a drink."

"Do you think that he dislikes you?"

"No." The girl took the cat into her lap and stroked it and looked thoughtful. "I think Uncle John is just the kind of man who gets tired of people. Anybody, I mean. He just can't be bothered to keep up being nice."

"I see," Miss Rachel said, writing briefly. "And what does your uncle do in a business way?"

"Sells stocks and bonds in an office downtown. He's been there for years. I guess he's a sort of vice-president, or something. The firm is called Tewsley, Tewsley, and Dunn."

"I believe that takes care of your uncle except for one item. Have any of these—accidents, we'll call them—taken place during hours when he could not have arranged them? I mean, for instance, some mischief done when he was at the office."

"I don't know. I'd have to think about that."

"Do, then, while we go on with the others. Your aunt, let's say."

"My aunt's name is Lydia. She's about forty, I suppose, but she looks young and pretty when she's fixed up. Oh, but it couldn't have been Lydia who did these things. She's always been so nice about the accidents, even when something she liked very much had been broken."

"Hmmmmm. . . ." Miss Rachel made spidery dark writing on the page. "Go on, then."

"There's Lee. She's my cousin. She's beautiful the way a doll is, only more alive and intelligent. She's twenty-one and has the most beautiful pale hair you can imagine." The girl's face, bent above the cat, was suddenly unhappy. "I guess you'd say that Lee was perfect. She just has everything."

Miss Rachel was watching from the corner where the desk stood. "And how does she act toward you?"

"Oh . . ." The girl shrugged. "All right. We don't have much in common. She's going to college, you see. I guess in her mind I'm just a Middle West hick."

"I'm sure that no one would think of you that way," Miss Rachel said, watching the sensitive profile, the smudged, tired marks under the eyes where the wet traces of tears still glittered. "Does your cousin ever help you with these chores of yours?"

"She rearranges the furniture once in a while."

"And dusts it, then?"

"No. I do that."

"I see. Is there anyone else?"

"Oh yes. Two. My two other cousins. One is Lee's brother, my uncle's son. His name is Thaw. He's about twenty-five. He was in the Navy and was hurt so badly in an explosion just after Pearl Harbor was attacked that he was discharged. He's been there ever since I have. I like him, though he's a little bit hard to know. Sometimes I think he broods over being laid up like he is—he was hurt pretty badly, you see—and that he gets nervous and tired and snaps at people without meaning to."

"And your other cousin?"

"He's"—the girl seemed to find difficulty with her voice—"he's the way I am. He does chores, the gardening work and little repairs, and washing the cars, and things like that."

"He is your uncle's second son?"

The girl raised startled eyes. "Oh, not at all! He's like me, you see, a poor relative they've taken in to help. Only they've had him since he was ten, and I guess the niceness wore off years ago."

"If there was any," Miss Rachel murmured. "How does he treat you?"

"Pete has just been wonderful," the girl said softly. "I think he knows, sometimes, what's going on; that perhaps he has an idea about it. It was Pete, you see, who thought I should come to see you."

"Pete sounds like a very sensible young man," Miss Rachel agreed. "Now. About your little bird. Did you see anyone touch his cage today?"

"No. My aunt was in my room—she keeps towels and things stored in my dresser—but I don't know of anyone else who would have even gone near him."

"If you will leave your bird with me I think I can find out, by having his body analyzed, just what it was that killed him. As for these other things . . ." Miss Rachel nibbled absently at the end of her penholder and studied the wall. "What about the servants?"

"It couldn't be the cook, and she's all that's left. They've had three cooks while I've been there, and the accidents were going on during the time the changes were made."

"It's not likely the cook is to blame, then," Miss Rachel said. She put down the pen and swung about in her chair so that she was facing the girl. "I'm going to think over very carefully what you've told me, and I will make other inquiries too. Meanwhile, I wish you to be quite careful in everything you do. Stay with a group or two or more in your uncle's house whenever it is possible. Lock your door at night and prop a chair under the knob. Like this."

Miss Rachel went swiftly to the hall door and demonstrated the old-fashioned methods of security.

The girl seemed suddenly pale. She had half risen out of her chair, letting the cat drop; her lips were taut, trembling. "You believe it, then? You believe that someone hates me?"

Miss Rachel came to stand beside her, a Dresden figure in sprigged muslin, smelling of lavender, and with a face serene as an angel's. "The one thing you mustn't do, my dear, is to give way to fear. Sit down and be calm while I make us some tea. What I told you to do were merely sensible precautions. It is possible that someone dislikes you enough to do you harm."

"Why should they?" the girl cried passionately. "I've tried so hard to please, to make them like me, to—to belong to them—" She put a hand to her mouth to stop its trembling. "I've been so lonely. I wanted someone of my own."

"I know, my dear, and that brings up a request I have to make of you. I wish you wouldn't make any especial effort to please your uncle's family from now on. Do what you're supposed to do and no more, and what you do, do as if it were a chore you didn't relish particularly but simply wanted to get out of the way. Do you understand?"

The girl was staring at her strangely. "Be like that? Be ungrateful?"

A ghost of a smile tugged at Miss Rachel's lips. "With maids as they are, my dear, you've more than repaid any of their kindness."

"Very well," the girl said, hesitating. "I'll try it, anyway."

They were silent together over the tea, while the cat lay purring by the fire and the clock's ticking was the only interruption to the quiet. Miss Rachel, meanwhile, itemized the girl's clothing. The dark coat had belonged to someone else, someone with more of a flair for a severe and tailored cut than this girl would have. The girl cousin, Lee, perhaps. Miss Rachel visualized her as a lovely and faceless figure with pale floating hair, wearing the dark coat. Its strict cut would accent that type of beauty. The shoes and hose were cheap, the skirt and linen blouse bought for service and not appearances. The veil, Miss Rachel thought, must have been Shirley Grant's idea. It was typically the romantic type of headgear that eighteen-year-olds would love.

Shirley Grant broke the silence suddenly by saying: "Do you know, I forgot to tell you about Addison."

Miss Rachel put aside her cup. "Addison?"

"Addison Brill, Aunt Lydia's brother."

"Does he live with the family?"

"Part of the time. Most of the time, lately." Some trace of embarrassment had come into her expression; she had colored a little, and her eyes avoided Miss Rachel's. "I suppose I left him out because I try so hard not to think about him."

Miss Rachel's glance was sympathetic, but she made no attempt to hurry Shirley Grant to go on.

"He—he drinks so much, and when he's drunk he's so uncouth and silly. Sometimes when he's awfully drunk he pretends to be in l-love with me. I always go then and sit in the bathroom till he's gone. He isn't at all neat or careful of his appearance like the rest of the family. He's just—impossible to be around. I wonder sometimes how they stand him."

The gas muttered faintly; Samantha, the cat, gave forth a prodigious yawn.

"I suppose," Shirley went on quietly, "that they let him stay because he has so much money and he's just about ready to die."

3

Miss Rachel sat quite still for a moment. It was then, she thought later, that an inkling of the terror to come on Chestnut Street first stirred in her mind; a faint chill settled on her neck, and the ticking of the clock seemed distorted by the silence of the room into a hoarse and pulselike hammering.

She took a steadying breath. "Ready to die? In what way?"

"He has an alcoholic heart, or some such thing. Uncle John said once that Addison was apt to pop off at any moment, and if he did he wanted to see him cremated because all that liquor was going to burn like the devil."

There was no sign of humor in the girl's sober face.

"Your uncle seems a bit on the macabre side, so far as fun goes," Miss Rachel said. "However, do you think that Addison might be the type to work these mischiefs? He might be quite piqued, you know, by your going off to sit in the bathroom."

The girl shook her head. "He's the one person I am sure just couldn't have done any of these things. He wasn't even living at the house when the trouble started, and one of the things broken was a bottle of expensive scotch whisky. Addison in his blottiest moments wouldn't break a bottle of that."

"I see." Some ghost of trouble still nagged at Miss Rachel's thought. "You said, didn't you, that he had a great deal of money? If he dies, who gets this?"

The girl looked at her blankly. "I don't know. Aunt Lydia, I suppose, since she's his sister and he hasn't anyone else that I know of."

For a while there was silence while Miss Rachel resumed the sipping of her tea and the girl sat waiting. "One last thing," Miss Rachel said finally. "Since this young man you call Pete had the idea first of coming to see me, I should like to talk to him too. Suppose you ask him to come here sometime tomorrow afternoon."

"I'll tell him," the girl said.

At the door she paused to look out at the night. The pavement that wound downward between vacant properties, the grasses parched by summer, the bisecting corner of Chestnut Street were stark under the moon. The shadow of the curbing was like a line drawn in black crayon; the roof of Miss Rachel's porch made a shape on the sidewalk like the silhouette of a hat.

"How still everything is!" the girl murmured, "and—lovely, isn't it?"

"I don't believe I've ever seen moonlight as brilliant," Miss Rachel agreed, but she wondered privately if the girl should have come out in so bright a light.

She was still in the parlor somewhat later, sitting at her little desk and looking at the sheets of paper she had written upon, when Miss Jennifer came in.

Miss Jennifer was puffing somewhat more than usual, it seemed, and she dropped the Parchly Heights Methodist Ladies' Aid account book on the floor with a loud slam before she put it on the hall table. Then she asked in a voice that seemed breathless and weak: "Are you still up, Rachel?"

Miss Rachel opened her mouth and then shut it again, which she knew was wrong of her, and waited in silence until Miss Jennifer came to the living-room door.

Miss Jennifer jumped and gave a gasp when she saw her. "Rachel! Can't you answer when you're spoken to? Dear, you gave me a start."

"Why, Jennifer? Why should I have startled you?"

Miss Jennifer stood still, and a cautious look came into her face. She was, in Miss Rachel's opinion, somewhat discomposed and flustered, and the rakish angle at which her hat hung over one eye was strictly out of character for Jennifer.

"What's wrong with you?" Miss Rachel wondered. "Nothing at all," Miss Jennifer got out, and advanced toward the mantel, where she usually put her spectacles in their case, and then stopped and looked dazedly at each of her hands.

Nothing was lost on Miss Rachel. "What's become of your glasses?"

"I—I don't know."

"You have lost them," Miss Rachel decided. "How could you, Jennifer, on the short walk from Mrs. Brenn's?"

A sort of righteous determination came into Miss Jennifer's expression, and she closed her lips firmly on whatever answer she had intended to make; Miss Rachel was reminded of the time she had taken Jennifer to see the exhibition of nudes at the art galleries. Miss Jennifer, like a mule, had her balking point, and this was it. Miss Rachel made her tone quite casual and said, "Oh well, in the dark one is apt to lose things easily anyway."

Miss Jennifer couldn't resist the correction. "It isn't dark outside. It's—it's sort of unnatural. The moonlight, I mean."

"Oh?" Miss Rachel made a deliberate chore of getting her notes together. "I hadn't noticed."

"You can see everything with a dreadful distinctness," Miss Jennifer went on, as though the words were being forced out of her. "Every house, every bit of lawn and garden, every gate and hedge and—and step is just as clear as though it were day." She shivered suddenly, which Miss Rachel seemed not to see, and went on: "I wish that I had come home much earlier. Finding the error about the fifty-eight cents wasn't worth it."

"Wasn't worth what?" said Miss Rachel absently.

The righteous determination came into Miss Jennifer's face again; she sat down on the chair the girl had vacated and began to remove her gloves. The silence was punctuated by the ticking of the clock like a series of little question marks.

Rachel said, again very casually: "What is the number of Mrs. Brenn's house on Chestnut Street?"

Miss Jennifer gave her a wary glance before answering. "Thirteen thirty-nine is Mrs. Brenn's address. Why?"

"Did you by any chance notice any of the houses on the opposite side of the street? One in particular; it's a trifle this side of Mrs. Brenn's address. Thirteen-fifty. A rather nice house, I should think."

Miss Jennifer's mouth had dropped open, and she was staring at Miss Rachel in what was obviously terror.

"Someone went inside it, perhaps, while you were walking past," Miss Rachel went on, thinking of Shirley Grant and not liking the queer appearance which had come over Jennifer.

"You can't possibly know about that!" Miss Jennifer choked. "You can't! I won't believe that you do!"

"Were you nervous?" Miss Rachel asked, remembering Shirley's humble manner, which might look like skulking under the moonlight.

"Nervous!" wailed Miss Jennifer.

"There is something going on inside that house," Miss Rachel said ominously, "which makes me afraid. A pattern of frightfulness which began small and is growing bigger; a mean and clever intelligence which has turned at last to death."

She was thinking of the canary, wrapped in the man's handkerchief, tucked into a drawer of her desk.

Miss Jennifer tottered up out of the chair and fled for the hallway. Miss Rachel sat, amazed, and heard her running steps on the stairs and wails which came intermittently like the cries of a child in the deep dark. She listened for the slamming of Miss Jennifer's bedroom door, and when it came she, too, went upstairs.

But there was no getting Miss Jennifer out of bed. She was crouched under the bedding with all lights on, shivering as if with cold, and when Miss Rachel peeped under at her she made a chattering remark about witches and a request that Miss Rachel go away.

"You've meddled with it so long," Miss Jennifer got out as Miss Rachel paused at the door, "that you've gotten psychic about it. You know it before it happens. You're—" She sneezed with the nervous beginnings of a cold. "Go away! I won't say anything more!"

Miss Rachel went downstairs again, turned out the gas, tested the window fastenings, went with the cat for her nightly chore out of doors. Standing and looking at the moon as she had with Shirley Grant, she thought: "*It?* What does Jennifer mean by *it?*"

She went back over Miss Jennifer's return to the house, the dropping of the book, her jumpiness on suddenly seeing Miss Rachel, the terror she had shown over the questions about the house on Chestnut Street, and came to an inevitable conclusion. Something had happened to frighten Jennifer out of her wits, and that something might still be going on now.

She went back to the hall closet and returned to the front porch wearing a little plush cape and a dark hat pulled down over her white hair. Calling the cat produced no results; Samantha had seen the hat and was evidently in a mood to follow. Resigned to the cat's company, Miss Rachel walked quickly away in the direction of Chestnut Street. She was at the corner when the first wail of a police siren lifted itself into the night.

Miss Rachel stood still, and in the silence following the scream of the siren she heard the rustle of the cat scampering under the hedge that bordered the sidewalk, and the croak of a little frog, a soft and lonely sound in the quiet of the garden.

She began to hurry; at the corner opposite Mrs. Brenn's garden she paused again to take in the bunched collection of cars, the hurrying men, the confusion and lights at 1350 Chestnut Street, and with a practiced eye she picked out the black sedan belonging to Detective Lieutenant Stephen Mayhew of the Homicide Division.

She studied then the surroundings of the house. There was a tall hedge between it and this next house to the corner. Without any scruples that she was conscious of, Miss Rachel swung open the white picket gate and cut diagonally across the intersecting lawn. Though there were lights on here next door, there was no one looking out. The people inside were either overly polite, or their curiosity had been satisfied. In an effort to satisfy her own, Miss Rachel made prickly progress through the hedge and came out into the yard of 1350.

Before her was a strip of turf, a flagged pathway, and a bed of night-blooming stock. The colors of the flowers made a pastel border against the white wall of the house. There was a window, also, its sill just at eye level, the lower frame raised so that the curtains moved softly with the air from outside. The room beyond was dark.

Miss Rachel stole toward the front of the house and found herself looking at the broad back of a uniformed officer who stood twiddling a night stick and whistling "Moonlight and Roses" very softly, as though affected by the brilliance of the moon.

Miss Rachel retreated to the rear, passing other windows whose shades were down with lights behind them, and was about to step upon the broad porch there when voices reached her from just inside the back screened door. She dropped out of sight behind an oleander bush and waited until the voices were gone. Samantha came and rubbed the sprigged muslin with a hard inquisitive ear and sharpened her claws on the wood of the steps.

Miss Rachel went back to the first window and tried to peer in.

There were faint odors of tobacco, of leather, the indefinable dry smell of books. Miss Rachel tested the pane with her finger tips, and it rose easily in its channel. She stood on tiptoe and put her head in and made out the vague shape of a big desk and bookshelves and a mantel with a deer's head over it. This would be a man's room, she thought. She turned and looked about at the limited space between the house and the hedge.

A torrent of white roses spilled from the top of a fanshaped trellis beyond the bed of stock. Miss Rachel, investigating, found the wood of the trellis stout, its construction admirable. It took a while and some soil on the sprigged muslin to dig it out of the earth and to unfasten the rose branches from the wood. Then some practice was necessary before the correct balance was obtained at a spot under the window. Getting a little precariously over the sill, Miss Rachel made up her mind to call to the attention of Lieutenant Mayhew the ease with which trellises might be put to the uses of burglars.

The cat made the window ledge in a single leap and stood there purring and watching Miss Rachel, who had moved off through the gloom. When her eyes had become accustomed to the dim light Miss Rachel saw that the room had two doors, one at either end. She opened the nearest door a crack; a span of yellow light illumined the darkness, and Miss Rachel put an eye to it.

A group of people sat in what was obviously a dining room. The center of the space was taken up with a large table, on which was a centerpiece of crystal flowers and little deer, reflecting the light from the hanging fixture above. The chairs in which the people sat were pushed away, arranged in clusters.

Ash trays littered the edge of the table, and blue smoke trailed in the bright light.

Shirley Grant sat quite alone in a near corner. She still wore the blue coat and the veil upon her hair, but she looked more pinched, more tired than ever, and her eyes were dry and held a fixed, stunned appearance.

Two people opposite her, ignoring her, were older than the others. Mentally Miss Rachel labeled them as Mr. and Mrs. Terrice. The woman was blonde, with pale skin carefully rouged, a petulant, proud look to the pose of her head, immaculately slim hands with fuchsia-tinted nails toying with a cigarette in a holder. She was at least forty, the kind of forty that stays beautiful because it is fragile and not fat.

The man was small and neat. His eyeglasses and his half-bald head added, somehow, to the impression of neatness; the glasses shone with cleanliness, and the bald head looked sleek and tended. He had a narrow, rather expressionless face on which the brows were unexpectedly heavy. He was tapping out a cigar into a tray.

At the far end of the table two young people sat with their elbows upon the wood. The girl's pale hair was dressed in a style so elaborate as to be almost painful; there was an arched pompadour, a topping of curls, a long and twisted roll from temple to shoulder. Framed by this formal and stylized glory was a rounded, delicate, utterly beautiful face. The effect was that of a doll put up to be displayed. Or of a Renaissance angel in a painting.

Beside her was a young man with a square face, dark eyes, heavy brows reminiscent of Mr. Terrice's, a stubborn chin on which a deep scar had made a triangular incised mark.

The girl said something in an undertone, and the young man shook his head; there was an effect of distaste and impatience in his movement. These two, Miss Rachel thought, would be the Terrice younger generation: Lee, the girl, and Thaw, her brother.

Thaw, Miss Rachel remembered, was possessed by a chronic snappishness since his injury in the Navy. Lee was the modern young sophisticate, glittering and blasé.

Mr. Terrice had finished extinguishing his cigar. He pulled his coat straight, turned in his chair to face Shirley in her corner. He didn't quite meet her eyes; he seemed to be examining some detail in the wall behind her. "I want to be as fair as I can, Shirley. Understand that I'm not making an accusation. But we deserve the truth."

The girl seemed to crouch, to grow thinner, smaller.

"I want to know," John Terrice went on, his face as expressionless as ever, "just why you were hiding a bullet in your hand when I met you in the hall tonight."

4

"BUT YOU'RE mistaken, Uncle John. I wasn't hiding it. I mean, I didn't intend to hide it. There wasn't any reason I should have." She seemed to take in the curious silence of the others. "Was there?" she stammered.

Mr. John Terrice adjusted the crease of one trouser leg; his wife flicked ash off her cigarette with a tap of a fuchsia nail.

"You know, my dear," Lydia Terrice said, "that you brought me a box of blanks. Not just one."

"I went back," Shirley said quickly. "I remembered that you had said you wanted the box."

The square-faced young man with the scar on his chin, staring at the crystal deer, said idly, "Addison was pretty rotten to you, wasn't he, Shirley?"

"Not—not *that* rotten," Shirley said. "I wouldn't have killed him."

The silence came back for some moments. Mr. John Terrice spent the time in wiping his glasses.

Lydia Terrice spoke again. She had a soft, controlled voice with an amused inflection as artificial as the fuschia nails. "I'd never realized what sort of people policemen were before. I'd thought of them as sort of brave automatons who chased robbers." She watched the smoke rising from her cigarette. "That Lieutenant What's-his-name—Mayhew, I think—is pretty shrewd. He's far from being a robot. I don't believe I'm going to like him."

Lee gave the other woman a flickering smile; the effect was as if a lovely and expensive doll had looked back interestedly from inside its glass case. "He was rude, darling, to tell you your little trick on Addison was stupid."

"He hadn't breathed Addison's alcoholic miasma as long as we had," Thaw flung out, "or he'd have rigged up a shotgun loaded with grape."

John Terrice had put on his glasses and was looking at his son. "I'll have to remind you, Thaw, that remarks of that sort are very much out of order. Addison has been murdered. The police are apt to be quite a nuisance until the murderer is discovered. Things such as you have just said won't make conditions any more pleasant for anyone."

In resentment at his father's correction Thaw began to grind out a cigarette as though trying to bore a hole in the bottom of the ash tray.

Lee put a hand on his impatient one. "Dad's right; it isn't the smart thing to remember Addison's faults. It might not be even too bright to think about the money he left us. We did a dim-witted trick in fixing up the gun to scare him; let's act sorry about that. And let's give out with as little personal stuff for the police and newspapers to mull over as possible."

Thaw laughed, a sudden and humorless sound. "The fuss they make over a cluck like Addison—ready to drop in his tracks from heart trouble, drinking himself to death on top of that— makes me sick. He was my uncle. So what? I've seen better men than Addison die by hundreds, and no damned detectives on the scene, either."

"What you say is quite true," John Terrice answered carefully. "And yet, for the safety of the rest of us, you are going to have to acquire a different perspective on this matter. You have been at war, and certain things in civilian life seem trivial to you now." John Terrice straightened a cuff inside his sleeve with critical nicety. "The feeling of triviality would vanish if Lydia or Lee should happen to be arrested for Addison's death. Think of that possibility and you won't be nearly as careless in your opinions."

He had made an impression. Thaw looked at the delicate girl beside him, at the small and graceful figure of Mrs. Terrice. "I'll keep my mouth shut," he said finally with curtness.

Mrs. Terrice put in, in her voice with its subdued and brittle amusement: "I agree, John, that Thaw should use a little care in his speech. But your picture of Lee or of me being arrested for murder is a trifle out of focus, is it not? That Lieutenant— Mayhew—knows about the revolver in the niche at the entry. I explained to him that it had been loaded with a blank, put there to frighten Addison for a joke when he came home from his drinking bout. Only I didn't call it a drinking bout, of course, or let on how really tired we were of Addison's staggering in at all hours. I made it sound like a silly prank that had accidentally gone wrong. I think that's much the most likely story for the police. It was a joke, and it came off wrong, and no one is to blame for Addison getting killed. No one at all."

The curious silence returned, and after a moment Miss Rachel saw that John Terrice was looking again at Shirley Grant.

"The police are a peculiarly suspicious lot, and you were right in judging Lieutenant Mayhew to be shrewd," he said some minutes later. "In the brief talk I had with him he asked me if there had been much chance of a genuine bullet getting exchanged for the blank you meant to use, and I told him there hadn't been any chance at all."

Lydia Terrice looked as though he had just slapped her.

"I told him the chance of an accident was quite improbable, because there wasn't a real bullet in the house."

The cat was rubbing Miss Rachel's ankles on the other side of the slit in the door, and the sound of her purring was like that of a tiny motor running at high speed. The air that blew in through the open window was warm with the summer night, and yet the purring of the cat was not homely or familiar enough, the air not warm enough, to keep Miss Rachel from feeling strange and chilled.

The conversation in the other room was moving slowly toward some preconceived point. Miss Rachel felt the pattern of it; the cautious knitting up of a net to catch the victim.

"But you've spoiled what I said, then!" Lydia Terrice cried, forgetting to be amused, and Lee Terrice was staring at her father strangely.

"Perhaps I have," John Terrice said smoothly, "in some respects. True, you thought that you were putting a blank shell into the gun, when you were undoubtedly putting in a live one, and so from your point of view Addison's death was an accident and you were wise to stress that opinion to the police. But this man Mayhew is far too clever not to investigate other things about that bullet. Such as how you came to have it."

"But"—she made an impatient gesture—"you have heard how I happened to have it. Shirley brought it to me from the closet upstairs. Lee and Thaw and I were together in the den. I put the bullet in the gun in front of all of them, and Thaw took the gun out to the entry, with Lee and I following, and fixed the trigger with a string so that the gun would go off when Addison opened the door."

He bent toward her, his sleek head inclined as if to listen intently to what she would say. "And the bullet you selected—was it different in any way from the others?"

"I don't know. I didn't see the others." She was staring now at Shirley.

"Didn't see them?" he echoed.

"Shirley took one from the box and handed it to me, and I put it in the gun."

"Did you ask her to do this?"

"No. Well—perhaps I may have."

"You had better remember that point more definitely," he warned, "or the lieutenant will badger you about it."

"I don't believe that she had asked Shirley to do this," Lee put in. "I seem to remember Shirley standing a trifle behind us all, reaching through with a bullet in her fingers when Lydia asked for one."

As though he had settled some phase of the questioning to his satisfaction, Mr. Terrice turned again to Shirley. "Let's go back over our meeting in the hall, my dear. When I met you you were coming away from your room. Is that where the box of blanks had been stored?"

Lydia answered at once, as though the trivial point annoyed her: "Of course it wasn't. I sent Shirley to the linen shelves off the upstairs bath—that storage space beside the shower. That's where she got the bullets."

"No, it wasn't where I got them," Shirley corrected, thoroughly confused. "After I'd looked through all of the linen shelves I remembered that often you stored extra things in the dresser in my room, and I went to look. There they were, as I had thought they might be. I started out with one." She turned to Mr. Terrice. "I met Uncle John in the hall, and just after I'd passed him I remembered that you had asked for the box, so I went back."

"And you brought the box of blanks downstairs?" Mr. Terrice asked.

"Yes."

"Then why, my dear," he pounced coldly, "didn't you offer *the box of blanks* to your aunt?"

"I don't know." The dry-eyed look she turned on him was puzzled and miserable. "Aunt Lydia said something like, 'Give me a shell now,' and I must have forgotten about offering the box."

The calmness of Mr. Terrice was akin to that of a surgeon using a scalpel. "And then you did—what?"

She stared at her finger tips twined in her lap. "I—I put away the box of shells."

"Put them back into your room?"

"No." She waited until his silence, his waiting, compelled her to finish. "I left them in the pantry. That's where the police found them."

"I came into the den just as the others returned from fixing up the unfortunate little surprise for Addison," Mr. Terrice said, suddenly leaning back with an effect of relaxing, "and I don't recall seeing you there for the rest of the evening. What happened to you?"

Her eyes made a frightened circuit of the room; she was obviously and transparently trying to make up a lie. "When I— when I went into my room for the shells I noticed my little bird was acting ill. After I had put the shells into the pantry I went down into the cellar where Pete was. He had an electric iron all apart and was trying to find what was wrong with it."

"That's right," Lee added absently. "I asked him to fix the iron so that I could press a formal. My blue one."

"And then?" Mr. Terrice said.

"He went upstairs with me and we tried to give the bird a little water with a spoon, and it—it finally died."

Lydia said in a tone that might have been one of genuine sympathy: "Oh, Shirley, what a shame!"

Shirley bit a lip before she went on. "Then Pete went back to his work and I—I stayed there in my room. I just wanted to be alone."

"Of course," Lydia said. "You poor child. Your poor little bird!"

"Curious," Mr. Terrice said meditatively. And then: "Might I see your bird, Shirley?"

"I—I buried him," Shirley stammered.

Mr. Terrice raised his extraordinarily thick brows to show his surprise. "Out of doors, Shirley? At night?"

She didn't look at him. "Yes."

"You weren't, by any chance, out of doors at the time Addison was shot?"

"I was just at the back door," she said quickly. "Just coming inside."

"Don't you feel free to use the front entrance?"

"Yes—only, you see, no one knew I'd been out, and I thought it would save questions—and things—if I just slipped back—" She stumbled in what she was trying to say. "I don't mean that I was trying to keep anything a secret—"

"How did you know then," Mr. Terrice cut in, "that the sound you had heard was Addison being shot?"

There was an instant of silence so complete that the purring of the cat rose into it like the sound of a miniature airplane, and Miss Rachel pushed the animal with her foot and was rewarded by being nipped at.

Shirley got out, "I didn't know about Addison. Not then. I heard a shot—I didn't know just where—and came through the house and found you all at the front door."

"The shot hadn't sounded right," Lydia said. "I knew at once something had gone wrong. I told John—"

Thaw Terrice suddenly said emphatically: "What's that damned thrumming noise? I hear it ever so faintly once in a while, like a motor running a long ways off."

He was looking directly at the door behind which Miss Rachel and Samantha were hidden, and John Terrice's expressionless eyes followed Thaw's and settled on it too.

Miss Rachel, seeing that cold glance, shivered. She stooped in the dark and reached for the cat, who evaded her with a sidewise leap that caused the door to click shut.

There was no time at all to be lost. Miss Rachel caught the tip of Samantha's tail, and Samantha escaped again by leaving a few hairs in Miss Rachel's hand. A chair scraped the floor of the dining room; Lydia's voice came, throaty with sudden nervousness.

Miss Rachel ran to the window and scrambled through it and was pushing the rose trellis down into the bed of stock when a light came on inside the room she had just left. Mr. Terrice, shorter even than she had supposed, now that she saw him standing, was in the door to the dining room. He brushed back an invisibly displaced lock of his thinning hair with the palm of one hand. With the other hand he pointed to Samantha.

"It's only a stray cat!" He gave something like a laugh.

Lydia, slim in diaphanous blue, slipped past him. At this distance she gave an impression of youth, of silky charm. "Horrors, it's a dreadful *black* cat! Aren't they symbolic of death or something? Scat! Drive it out, John. And how did it get inside in the first place?"

"Through the open window, obviously," Thaw snapped, coming over to draw down the pane.

Miss Rachel pressed herself into the prickly recesses of the hedge, felt fuzzy dust settle on her from its leaves, wondered if the sprigged muslin was apt to survive the night. The window framed the people in the room beyond: Thaw with his irritable eyes and his scar, Lee with her glittering hair, Lydia as small and as graceful as if she were sixteen, John Terrice all sleekness and composure. A frightened face peeped from the dining room and disappeared, and Miss Rachel felt disappointment well in her. She had hoped that Shirley might recognize the cat, might guess that the cruel questioning had had a listener who was her friend.

She was digging back through the hedge with an idea of waiting there until she could reclaim the cat, when something reached at her from the hedge's other side.

A hand. A hard cold hand that slid across her mouth.

5

"AND JUST what do you think you're doing?" said a gruff masculine voice in her ear. A young voice, edgy with tension. "And who are you, anyway?"

She bit him, and the hand jerked away, but a sudden hole enlarged itself in the hedge where he had pushed through to get at her, and she toppled back toward him. After an interval of clutching blindly at twigs and of hearing muffled groans, Miss Rachel found herself sitting on the lawn of the house next door. The moon, beginning to set, showed her a young man sitting facing her, who clutched one hand in the other and made grimaces suggestive of pain.

She got up and smoothed the sprigged muslin and straightened her wraps. "I'm sorry if I hurt you, but I don't like people who put their hands over my mouth out of the dark."

"I apologize," he groaned. "I deserve it, I guess. I should have found out who you were first. All I could see was a shape in the hedge. I didn't know who it was." He looked ruefully at his bitten hand.

"And you know now?" Miss Rachel asked, surprised.

He glanced at her. "Of course. You're Miss Murdock. Shirley went to see you tonight. I told her to go."

"Then you must be Pete," Miss Rachel said.

"Pete Whittemore, miss." He scrambled up, rubbed his bitten hand hard along the side of his shirt, and seemed to think it cured. He was light-complexioned, with sandy unruly hair and a manner of quirking his lips in what was not quite a smile but which gave the impression of a quiet and rather sardonic sense of humor. He quirked his lips at her now, and the moonlight turned eyebrows and lashes to silver and left his eyes in shadow, so that the effect was a little like an amused and mischievous mask.

She took in his nondescript shirt, his battered cords, the tennis shoes stained and blotted with grease. The Terrices, she thought, wasted little money on clothes for their charges.

"Have you been inside?" she asked. "Have you talked with the police?"

"Do you mean since Addison was killed? No. I heard the shot from the cellar, but I wasn't sure what it was—a backfire, maybe, or something else—and I went on putting away my tools until I heard the excitement start. Then I thought suddenly of Shirley; I thought she might have been in some accident or some sort of trouble, and I hurried upstairs. The cook was going to pieces in a kimono in the kitchen, and she hadn't seen Shirley, but she knew Addison had been shot. I somehow got the idea Shirley might still be with you."

Miss Rachel thought of Jennifer under the bedclothes. "You didn't—ah—go to my house, did you?"

"That's exactly what I did, and I beat on the door and rang the bell—it was rude as the devil of me, I know—but I kept on until somebody came. Finally a little old lady

THE CAT WEARS A NOOSE · 41

peeped out at me and offered to chop me into pieces if I put so much as a toe in the door. She had an ax in one hand and I thought, of course, she must know something of Shirley's troubles and Addison getting killed to be frightened that way, and I tried to talk to her."

"She wouldn't talk," Miss Rachel decided, knowing Jennifer.

"No. She said that she knew nothing of any man being killed and that she didn't intend to be questioned about it."

"You had mentioned this man's murder?" Miss Rachel said thoughtfully.

"No, I hadn't. She just seemed to know why I was excited—I guess I was pretty wild; I thought Shirley had vanished off the face of the earth—and she told me to go away and not to come back under any circumstances."

"And so you came back here? Did you just arrive?"

"Just now—and made the mistake of trying to see who was hidden in the hedge." He rubbed his hand as though an uneasy memory stung him. "Have you seen Shirley? Did you come here with her?"

"I thought it was time a few things were looked into," Miss Rachel evaded. "From what Shirley had told me, I thought something quite violent was apt to take place."

"You did?" he said admiringly.

"It was the pattern of the thing," she explained, "which worried me. Little meannesses getting bigger. Incidentally, what do you think of the series of accidents which seemed to have happened to things in Shirley's care?"

The silver eyebrows knitted in a frown. "I don't know. When she first told me about them—they hadn't been going on long then—I thought it might simply be imagination on her part. Then one day I saw Shirley put away a wet mop in the broom closet and a little later I ran across it on the back porch—draped over a pair of white pumps that Lee had cleaned and put out to dry. I knew then that the things Shirley had talked about were real—and that someone must hate her so much that they were willing to do these cheap dirty tricks to get her into trouble. I've been uneasy since. I've tried to keep watch and could never quite catch up with whoever was doing the mischief. Tonight when her little bird died I felt like kicking myself for being so stupid and helpless. And I thought of you. I thought maybe you'd help Shirley." He made an awkward motion with the bitten hand. "I'd heard you were—well—rather a nice person."

"Thank you," Miss Rachel said. "You were right in thinking I would try to help her, though of course I can't guarantee any chance of success." She stood thoughtful and silent for some moments. "I'm trying to think of some way to keep Mr. Terrice from doing what he is trying to do now."

The quirk disappeared; the mask with its silver brows grew quite still. "Just what is Mr. Terrice trying to do?"

"He is manufacturing a nice case against Shirley in the matter of the murder of Mr. Brill."

Knuckles bunched and showed hard-white under the moon. "He is, is he? I'm not going to take that. It's time that somebody—"

"No, you don't," Miss Rachel cautioned, twitching his sleeve with a sharp jerk. "You would be playing into his hands if you did anything violent. Taking a poke at Mr. Terrice and being in love with Shirley at the same time would just be answering his prayers."

He seemed to be breathing with difficulty. "How did you know I feel that way about Shirley?"

"I would if I were you," she decided. "Now be quiet while I follow an idea I'm getting."

He stood there, restless and nervy, while she thought it out.

At last: "I believe I'll use Jennifer," she said.

"Jennifer?"

"My sister," she explained. "This is going to be rather illegal, and it may cause her some grief, but in a way she deserves it."

"I don't understand," he said.

"We are going to hunt for a case with spectacles in it. The case is somewhere along this sidewalk, or the one in the next block. It may have fallen under a shrub or into the gutter. I can't be sure, even, which side of the street it is on, but I believe that curiosity, at least, would have brought her fairly near and that it will be on this side."

"A spectacle case with glasses in it," he said with an air of unquestioning obedience. "And we'll have to keep out of sight of the police."

"I will, I think, though later you are going to have to brave them to find my cat for me. Now. Be quiet and be thorough." She led the way, stopping at a small shrub near the sidewalk to peer under it, and with a look toward the Terrice home to make sure that no police were watching, she went out through the picket gate to the street.

They searched, and the moon waned, and the lights and activity of the police receded gradually into the distance.

Miss Rachel raised, feeling the crick in her back from bending so long, feeling the sting of tiredness in her eyes. "I'm afraid—" she began, and just then Pete Whittemore cut her off.

"Got it!" He pounced upon a shadow where a white-flowering shrub overhung the edge of a lawn. "And the glasses are in it. Look. Is this the right spectacle case?"

With a faint twinge of guilt Miss Rachel saw in the dying light the old-fashioned gold frame and the small bifocal lenses of Jennifer's spectacles. "Yes, it's the right case." She hesitated while the memory of Jennifer's terror under the bedclothes made a brief plea for mercy.

"And what do we do now?"

Miss Rachel turned firmly to the thought of Jennifer's perfidy in not telling her immediately about the murder. "We'll plant these glasses under the nose of the police. In the shrubbery near the front entrance to Mr. Terrice's house, for instance."

"Don't you imagine that the police have already examined the ground pretty thoroughly? Suppose they don't believe these glasses are a clue?"

"There is one infallible way of making the police believe anything, and that is to pretend that you're trying to hide whatever it is from them," Miss Rachael instructed. "Take these glasses and drop them in some convenient spot, and when you're sure that an officer is looking at you pick them up quickly and put them in your pocket."

"Then they'll suspect me."

"For a moment, perhaps. They'll want to know why you picked the glasses up and tried to get away with them, and you can say—" She frowned briefly in thought, remembered suddenly the immaculate spectacles of Mr. Terrice. "You can say that you thought they might be your uncle's and you were just going to take them in and ask him. The police will then seize on the glasses and try to find out who owned them—which they will, of course, through the optometrist who made them. And it will be Jennifer."

He worried about it. "Won't that be rather hard on her? They might be nasty about it."

"I think that Jennifer will be able to take care of herself. The idea is to give the police someone to work on besides Shirley, whom I suspect is going to be nominated for their attention by Mr. Terrice. Jennifer will do as a stopgap."

"I feel sorry for her," he protested.

"She's the one who offered to work on you with an ax," Miss Rachel reminded. "Now get along and do what I told you to do. When you're quite finished answering questions you might locate my cat and bring her home to me. She's entirely black and she won't scratch you if you give her a bite to eat before you pick her up."

He looked at the spectacle case uneasily. "You know, I still don't feel quite right, involving a little old lady in something she didn't do."

"Don't be too sure about Jennifer," Miss Rachel said, walking away toward her own corner.

She wanted to be alone, to think over the events and the personalities of the evening and to add to her notes about Shirley Grant. And to figure, too, some way to wriggle herself innocently into the investigation made by the police. The police had certain resources of equipment and intimidation which Miss Rachel perpetually envied them, though she had found in previous affairs that having observed life and humanity for the space of seventy years was no mean advantage, either.

She wondered what Lieutenant Mayhew had discovered thus far, and what he was doing at the moment, and whether his square brown face was looking at Shirley Grant with the deceptive mildness which he reserved for his prize suspects.

Detective Lieutenant Stephen Mayhew came and stood in the door of the dining room, which he filled with the effect of a brown bear at the opening of its den, and regarded with deep thought the group of people who were settling themselves in chairs about the table.

"I'm sorry that we've had to keep you out of the living room," he said with the same effect, now vocal, of a bear trying to be amiable. "You may come back, now."

He stood aside and they filed past him. Mayhew wondered why they seemed to have just been seating themselves after so long a while in the dining room; his eye settled on the door to a room he knew now was the den, and from the lights being on beyond the open door, he decided that they had for some reason gone into the other room. He didn't like it. He wanted suspects who stayed put and kept their mouths shut; and this group, having gone in a body to the other room without consulting him, looked queer, looked like a mutual doctoring of evidence or something equally reprehensible. He decided to investigate the den thoroughly later.

The living room was a long, elegant room furnished in pastels. Two sofas faced each other on either side of a fireplace of gray fieldstone; the sofas were in coral, the string rug between them in soft, dull yellow. The dull yellow was repeated in the brocade of draperies at the windows, in a touch of detail in the pale wallpaper, in two figurines of china on the mantel. The room had not the used and lived-in look of the den. It was a little frosty for comfort, a little too fragile for ease, and the wide floor and the delicate furnishing gave rather the impression of a display, a model not meant to be used.

Mayhew saw that each of them, as they entered, cast a look at the recessed entry where the front door now stood closed. Mr. Terrice looked at it as though it annoyed him, and Mrs. Terrice looked at it and put up a spider-web handkerchief to catch a non-existent tear, and the three younger people just stared.

"Will you sit down over here, please?" Mayhew said, indicating the furniture that enclosed the space before the fireplace. "There are a few things I'll have to get straight, and then we'll call it a night."

"We've answered your questions till we're black in the face," Thaw flung out. "Can't you do your work without all this bungling around?"

Mayhew didn't answer this; he let them seat themselves and saw that Mr. and Mrs. Terrice took one of the coral sofas and that Lee Terrice took the other and that Thaw Terrice sank into a deep chair done in dove-gray velvet. The girl Shirley had begun to interest Mayhew; she seemed so frightened, so unnerved, so desperate for self-control. She took a small straight chair from its place by the wall and put it slightly behind the chair occupied by Thaw. It struck Mayhew that she was in this family without being part of it and that she was ill at ease in this room.

When they were settled Mayhew took a notebook out of his coat and leafed through it. He made no attempt to sit down, since the Terrice furnishings were not built to hold a man of his size, and he had no intention of trying a chair and of looking like a bear on a toadstool. He said: "What sort of financial shape was Mr. Brill in, Mr. Terrice?"

"I know very little about Addison's affairs," Mr. Terrice answered. "Once in a while he might ask me to pick him up a little stock at a bargain. He didn't confide in me otherwise."

"He didn't have to work for a living?"

"No. Addison had enough to live on." Mr. Terrice took out a white pocket handkerchief and touched his upper lip. "He had inherited some money from his family—from my wife's parents—years ago. He hadn't worked since."

This was going smoothly, Mayhew thought; he was getting a good picture of the murdered man: a drunk with plenty of money, for whom his family felt no grief, for whose going the cook was joyful though unstrung, and whose boorish love-making (also an item from the cook) must have been unendurable to a girl like Shirley Grant.

There was a scuffle, a brief outburst of words outside, and the door burst open and Edson, Mayhew's assistant, came in dragging another man. A slim, unruly-haired youngster of about nineteen, whose mouth was mocking before he made it still.

Edson held out something: a spectacle case in which glasses rested. "Found this guy trying to get away with these. He found them just beyond the porch. Thinks they might be Mr. Terrice's."

The room grew very silent, and Mr. Terrice stood up. He walked to Edson's outstretched hand and looked long at the glasses, and to Mayhew he seemed to grow a little pale. He turned his eyes on the tousled-haired young man, who scowled.

Even Mayhew, from where he stood, could see that the glasses in the open case were identical to the pair on Mr. Terrice's nose.

6

Miss Rachel looked out with interest at the day. Some clouds had come up since dawn, and the sky was full of a cool gray light, fuzzy at the horizons, and the big homes of Parchly Heights spread out below were massive and reserved, like a rich man at breakfast. Morning's quiet reproached her interest in violence.

Miss Jennifer peeped into the breakfast room. "Are you going to Aid Meeting this morning, Rachel? Wednesdays, you know."

Miss Rachel studied Jennifer's black cape, the hat with its blue flowers still a little awry, the Parchly Heights Ladies' Aid account book tucked solidly under one arm. "Haven't you located your glasses yet, Jennifer?"

"Not yet," Miss Jennifer said, and began to back away. "Don't go. I want to tell you something."

"I don't want to hear it," Miss Jennifer got out hastily. "I haven't time, I mean. I'm going to meeting."

"I wouldn't take *that*, if I were you," Miss Rachel said, pointing to the account book. "There's something peculiarly wrong with it."

Miss Jennifer cast a suspicious look at the book, then turned it over cautiously in her hands. She found shortly what Miss Rachel had seen: a spot of blood on the under cover. She gasped with shock and almost dropped the book; she looked at once small and angry and afraid.

"You may as well tell me about that man you saw murdered," Miss Rachel coaxed. "I know that you saw either the actual crime or the events immediately after it. When you came in last night you were—"

Miss Jennifer had fled with a slam of the front door; where she had stood lay the account book with the stained cover uppermost. Miss Rachel left the breakfast table and picked it up; she was still sitting and looking at it when Mrs. Marble, the housekeeper, came to say that there was a gentleman and he was carrying a cat.

"Bring him in," Miss Rachel directed absently. "I know who he is."

This did not seem to surprise Mrs. Marble, which should have warned her. When the housekeeper returned it was to usher in the large brown-coated and patient figure of Lieutenant Mayhew, carrying the cat.

Miss Rachel slid the account book out of sight upon an extra chair and asked him to sit down.

He sat down opposite her with a slow testing of the chair, which brought forth squeaks. The cat looked at her solemnly from over the top of the table; Mayhew pointed to the black ears with a big forefinger.

"Is this yours?" he asked.

Her face under its demure puff of white hair remained serene. "I don't know. It does look like my cat. Where did you find it?"

"I found it in a house in which a murder had just taken place," he said, "and the inference was obvious."

"What inference?"

"The inference that you had been there also. I know by now the habit your cat has of following you. It could hardly have come in alone."

"I haven't said," she pointed out, "that it is mine."

"In that case, perhaps I'd better take it to the city pound and let it be exterminated there."

They looked at each other for a long moment: the huge stubborn man and the little old lady as fragile as a doll.

"Your official mood isn't your nicest, and I don't like you in it," she said gently. Then after another moment: "And how is Sara these days?"

He shook his big head; his steel-gray eyes were cold. "No, you don't, Miss Rachel. You've played that tune too often. I know you saved my wife's life, and I've been grateful to you, and I've let you dabble in police business too many times because of it."*

She had the grace to blush a little. "Very well. I admit that the cat you found in the Terrice home was mine. I admit, too, that it had followed me inside. I know just how angry it must have made you when you found Samantha there. But, you see, I had a right to go prowling a bit—in a way."

He looked at her, impassive, disbelieving, and let the cat slide out of his arms to the floor.

"I can't have interference this time. I can't afford to. I'm up against something much too clever, much too adroit, to risk fumbling."

"You're up against something much too subtle to shut me

---

*   *The Cat Saw Murder,* The Crime Club, 1939.

out of it," she said. "I was, after a fashion, in on things before the murder happened. I can give you so much background, detail—"

He shook his head, stood up, bunched his hands inside his overcoat pockets. "I'm asking you to stay out of it. The thing's clever, but it's simple and straight. It was done with a trick, and when I know what the trick was I'll have the murderer. I don't want background and detail. I especially don't want the kind of slippery involvements that went on at Crestline."[†]

She said firmly: "But I have a right. I've been engaged by one of the people in that house."

"By whom?"

"By—Miss Grant." Seeing his start of attention, she hurried on: "The girl's been persecuted. She's the center of some kind of meanness, tricks meant to get her into trouble with the uncle and aunt. . . ."

A look almost of disgust had come into Mayhew's face. "The girl is neurotic. I can see that with half a glance. The others don't like her, and so she becomes persecuted. No, Miss Rachel, I can't have you on this. Leave it be."

"But Pete Whittemore backs her up. He told me these things were true, that her uncle seems to hate her, that someone is going out of their way to make her life miserable."

Mayhew stared at her now with marked attention. "You talked to this Pete Whittemore yesterday evening?"

"That's right."

"Did you and he plan any trick with a pair of glasses?"

Her eyes fled from his; she was painfully conscious of a blush beginning at her throat to steal upward. "I— Why do you mention this?"

[†] *Catspaw for Murder,* The Crime Club, 1943.

"Because Pete Whittemore was strangely able to find a pair of glasses in a case on ground I had recently searched. The case was sold by an optometrist who has among his clients your sister Jennifer. But the glasses in it were a pair of John Terrice's."

Miss Rachel watched her cat, who was investigating a saucer where milk was usually put. She saw what Pete had done: in reluctance to injure Miss Jennifer and in hatred of John Terrice, he had ruined the little plot about the glasses. There was now no connective link between the spectacles, the blot of blood on the account book, the snag in Jennifer's taffeta skirt (which might have torn on the Terrice's hedge), and any footprints and other evidence which the police might have gathered. Miss Jennifer could keep still with impunity, and Miss Rachel would be convicted in Mayhew's mind of the thing he hated most, the deliberate confusion of evidence.

"There might have been some error," she stammered.

"There was," he agreed. "It was the error of thinking that we were a little stupider than we are. No, Miss Rachel. It won't do. I forbid you"—he made it sound ominous and official—"I forbid you to meddle in the murder of Addison Brill. This is final, and I'm not apt to change my mind."

She had begun to get a little angry. "I must have some rights in this matter. Miss Grant came to see me before the murder occurred. She said that she was being persecuted and she asked me to help her. Do you mean that you can forbid me making an investigation on her behalf?"

"In such a case, no." He was colder, more remote, more stern than Miss Rachel ever remembered seeing him. "I cannot forbid you making an investigation of the matters relating to Miss

Grant." He waited, gave his next words deliberate emphasis. "I can and do forbid you to interrupt or to confuse the work of the police in the murder of Mr. Brill."

Miss Rachel, watching him, thought desperately: "We've been friends so long. . . . This can't be happening now. There's Sara—"

But before she could speak Mayhew went on: "Since you have, also, entered this investigation in the pay of one of the parties suspected of the murder, I forbid you to manufacture or conceal evidence relating to her possible part in the crime."

Miss Rachel cried: "But I wouldn't—!"

"You have," he reminded curtly. "Good-by, Miss Rachel." She watched him go, struggling between anger and regret, and for a long while after the front door had closed on his heavy step she sat quietly at the breakfast table. But when Mrs. Marble came with a second cup of coffee she refused it. She went instead to the hall closet for wraps, took the yellow ball of feathers from her desk drawer, still wrapped in the handkerchief, and put it into her purse. Then, by dexterously pushing Samantha with her foot at the last moment, she was able to leave the house without her.

She took the streetcar into town and went shamelessly to the police laboratories and asked for a friend of Mayhew's, Mr. Salter.

Mr. Salter, a dry little man with a sandy mustache, came and was sad about the bird—which he took to be Miss Rachel's, since she failed to tell him otherwise—and promised to do what he could about finding out why it had died.

As a last-minute thought Miss Rachel included the man's handkerchief. "I found it by the bird cage. I think it might be the—the gardener's." Lying was hard work for her, and not having a gardener at all made it worse; Miss Rachel felt fine perspiration come out across her upper lip. "He's queer, you know. He might have done it."

Mr. Salter said, "Hmmmm. . . ."

"He drinks," she added, remembering the details about Mr Brill.

"That's bad. Well, I'll do what I can for you. You might call me up sometime later today. Will you want your bird or shall I dispose of it?"

"That depends," Miss Rachel said thoughtfully. "You'd better keep it on hand until I tell you otherwise."

Leaving the police laboratories, she went to a drugstore and called the Terrice home. A frosty young voice answered her— Lee, she thought—and promised to bring Shirley if she could be found.

When Shirley came she sounded quiet and afraid. "Meet you downtown?" she said. "I'll see if I can get away."

"Quit repeating everything I say for the others to hear," Miss Rachel cautioned. "And why shouldn't you get away?"

"The cook is leaving," Shirley answered, "and I'm trying to run the kitchen. Aunt Lydia is calling the employment offices like mad, and they haven't anyone to send."

"I know," Miss Rachel said, remembering Mrs. Marble's hints about the wages paid in aircraft factories and Jennifer's outraged remarks at the twenty-five-dollar increase Miss Rachel had given her. "She won't find anyone, but that really isn't your responsibility. I want to talk to you. I suggest we have lunch downtown together. At the Tea Pot, say, in an hour."

"The Tea Pot in an hour," Shirley said dutifully, and Miss Rachel could have pinched her.

But Shirley seemed to be alone when she walked in forty-five minutes later and looked about for Miss Rachel. A waitress whom Miss Rachel had chosen for the look of intelligence about her approached Shirley and made sure who she was and then led her back to a far booth where the light was dim.

Shirley was dressed in a black wool suit with epaulets of silver fox grown a bit shabby and a gray hat trimmed with sequins. The outfit shrieked of Lee's streamlined sophistication.

"Why do you wear those things?" Miss Rachel asked impatiently, still cross over Shirley's break at the telephone. "Don't they ever buy you anything of your own?"

The sensitive face colored a little. "Not often. And Lee has such lovely things. . . ."

"For her. Not lovely on you, child. You should go in for pinafores and daisies. Besides, don't ever wear fur once it becomes ragged. There's nothing more untidy."

She sat there meekly, taking it in. Her very quiescence, her lack of fight, made Miss Rachel crosser than ever—until she remembered the mother's death, the girl's aloneness and lack of love.

"Look, my dear," she said gently. "I have been sitting here thinking over what you told me. There is a plan I want to try. It might work. With your co-operation and with Pete's I'm sure that it will."

"About how my bird died?" the girl asked. "I'd almost forgotten that, or that I asked you about it. Addison getting killed the way he did—"

"No, no," Miss Rachel corrected. "My plan is about your cook."

"The cook?" Shirley's eyes were startled.

"Yes. You see, it will be a way for me to get into your house and study things at first hand. To be the cook, I mean."

The girl's mouth sagged. "But you're so—so little and—well, you're sort of dainty and not—not young."

"You have no idea how desperate the shortage is in household help," Miss Rachel told her, "I spent the time before you arrived in talking over the phone to a few employment agencies. People are literally hiring anything that has two hands and isn't totally blind. I even frankly told one woman I was seventy, and she begged me to come in and register and promised a bonus if I got in before noon."

"I could help you with the heavy things," the girl said, still obviously trying to orient herself to Miss Rachel's idea. "And the meals there are very simple; they don't eat elaborately."

"I didn't think so," Miss Rachel agreed, remembering Lydia's slimness.

"But still—I'm just not that important. Not important enough for you to go to all this trouble."

"It isn't exactly trouble," Miss Rachel said with a wry look. "And Addison getting killed has made all sorts of confusion. The cook told Aunt Lydia about something she saw in the night, and Aunt Lydia said that she was crazy—it's more like a madhouse. You wouldn't like it. I can't ask you to do this for me."

"You didn't ask me," Miss Rachel pointed out. "And what was it the cook saw?"

A vague, unhappy fear came into the girl's face. "Something like a wolf, or the shadow of a wolf. She's foreign—she came from some country in the Balkans. Aunt Lydia says that she's insane, that people over here don't believe in things like that. I don't know. . . . I didn't like the part about it being outside my door."

Miss Rachel, studying the unhappy eyes, the white troubled face, said very quietly: "What was the part about it being outside your door?"

"Just standing and watching." The girl gave an uncontrollable small shiver. "As though it were waiting there for me to come out."

7

Miss Rachel asked incredulously: "Do you mean that the cook thought that she saw a werewolf?"

The girl glanced up in surprise. "Yes. That's what it was."

"There isn't any such thing," Miss Rachel told her. "There never has been."

She could not remember later feeling the slightest trace of fear. The idea of a werewolf in a house in Parchly Heights was so fantastic that it was funny. She simply didn't believe in the possibility of such a thing, Balkans or no Balkans, and trying to be frightened by it was like trying to be frightened of a witch on a broomstick.

"Foreign people are always thinking they see things like that," she went on, because the girl looked so miserable. "Middle Europe is ridden with old superstitions and odd beliefs. Just forget what the cook thought she saw. Your aunt is right: the woman is no doubt unbalanced—or at least on the verge of being queer."

"She didn't say," the girl added carefully, "that it was a werewolf. She said that it was the *shadow of a werewolf*."

"Substance or shadow—it was nightmare either way."

A little color seemed to come back into Shirley's face, and her shoulders moved as though, relaxing. "But your idea of trying to cook, Miss Murdock—I couldn't let you do that for me."

Miss Rachel was looking at her thoughtfully. "There is something about the house in which you live that worries me. No, don't look frightened again. I don't mean the super-natural. I mean the atmosphere, the feeling of the place—the dislike the family seems to have even for each other. Or perhaps it's just the way they struck me—as if they didn't belong together." She gave up trying to explain to the puzzled girl and sat staring at her cup of tea. "I want to get into that house, to stay in it night and day, and to find out why it strikes me so."

Shirley made no protest. She took a cake off the plate between them and nibbled at it and watched the new customers coming in to have luncheon at the Tea Pot.

"I think we shall use that waitress again," Miss Rachel decided, getting up. "She's an intelligent girl. Wait here until I come back."

She walked away, erect and small inside her best taffeta. When she returned the waitress who had approached Shirley at the door was following. Miss Rachel slid back into the booth and began to speak rapidly.

"I've already explained to this young lady," she said, indicating the waitress who stood by the table, looking amused, "that we were going to play a little joke on Mrs. Gerris."

Shirley almost dropped her cake. "Mrs. Gerris?"

"Mrs. Gerris," Miss Rachel said firmly. "And she has agreed to help us. Of course it's just for the birthday party and all in fun, but we do need help. We need someone whose voice Mrs. Gerris will not recognize. Now or later."

Shirley looked at the waitress in confusion, and Miss Rachel hurried on before she had time to ask a question.

"Now," Miss Rachel said, "we'll need Mrs. Gerris' telephone number."

She had to kick Shirley sharply under the table before the girl came awake enough to realize what was wanted. Shirley then gave forth with a Parchly Heights number, and Miss Rachel shepherded the two of them back to the telephone booths in the rear of the café.

It was a tight squeeze in the telephone booth. The waitress was beginning to be a bit surprised, and Shirley looked helpless and puzzled. Miss Rachel stayed in character as a funny little old lady with a yearning for practical jokes. She made chatter while the young waitress dialed. The sound of the telephone ringing at the other end of the line was a loud pulse in the stuffy booth.

The line opened with a snap, and a tiny voice crackled in the waitress's ear. Miss Rachel slipped the receiver over to Shirley.

"Who is it?" she whispered.

Shirley stared at her. "It's Lee."

"Ask for Mrs. Gerris," Miss Rachel told the waitress.

The waitress said, "Is Mrs. Gerris home? This is the employment agency calling."

The line was silent for a moment; came to life on a softer note.

"Mrs. Gerris?" the waitress asked. "I'm calling you from the agency. We have an applicant you might be interested in. Could I send her out to see you?"

The line said something in reply; the waitress put a hand over the mouthpiece and glanced at Miss Rachel. "She wants to know how old you are and how much experience you've had."

"Tell her I'm over fifty," Miss Rachel answered, "and that I'm a salad expert."

Listening to the rest of the conversation, Miss Rachel studied the profile of Shirley Grant where it was reflected on the glass panel of the booth. The downcast face was so shy, so unsure. She remembered Mayhew's bitter words: "The girl's neurotic—the others don't like her." She wondered irritatedly if there was any manner of magic which could rouse self-confidence in Shirley Grant.

The waitress hung up the receiver and turned away from the telephone. "You're to come out at once, and she'll give you an interview." Her eyes studied Miss Rachel's little figure. "You're going to be a shock. I can't imagine you doing anything more strenuous than making fudge."

Miss Rachel simpered, an expression she has found useful, and in the movement of getting out of the booth she managed to slip a bill into the girl's hand. "It's just a joke, of course, a funny little joke for Mrs. Gerris' birthday party. We're having loads of refreshments sent out, but she'll think for a little while that I made them."

"Oh, I see."

"Good-by, my dear, and thank you."

"Good-by." The waitress pocketed the bill and watched them walk away, and when Miss Rachel looked back at her from the front of the café she was still there, looking slightly amused.

Miss Rachel stopped in the shadow of a marquee and fanned herself with a lavender-scented handkerchief. "How hot it was in that booth! I thought we'd all suffocate. Did you understand, Shirley, why I used the name of Gerris?"

"I think so," Shirley said. "Wasn't it so that the waitress wouldn't recognize the name?"

"And it was enough like Terrice," Miss Rachel pointed out, "so that the change might not be noticed over the telephone. The waitress is a clever girl and she may decide later to investigate that telephone number, but I think for the present that we're safe. I have an appointment to see your aunt about being her cook. You must get home first and warn your young friend Pete. He might give things away if he saw me there unexpectedly."

Shirley made her last protest. "You've been so kind and patient. I can't let you go to all of this trouble about my little bird."

Miss Rachel stopped fanning to stare and remembered in time not to correct the impression which Shirley had just revealed. The child had no way of knowing, of course, just how curious she was about that hocus-pocus with the gun before Addison's arrival, or of how she had tried to involve Jennifer with the police to force her to talk.

"I know you've accidentally been involved in murder cases before," Shirley went on, "and those experiences must have been dreadful for you."

Miss Rachel gave forth with something between a choke and a sneeze. "I hadn't—um—thought of them that way, my dear. Now, we mustn't dally. You go along home and I'll follow in a little while."

Mrs. Terrice took her into the pantry, where the breakfast dishes still stood piled and stained with food. She indicated a pair of stools, and Miss Rachel sat down upon one.

Mrs. Terrice was in a morning gown of shell-pink chiffon. Her hair was tied on top of her head with a pink ribbon, and the mules she hooked on a rung of the stool were scarcely more than scraps of pink brocade. She was sixteen, Miss Rachel noted, everywhere but around her mouth, where slight lines had begun to tell the truth.

"The work isn't heavy, but I must be sure that you're capable of it," Mrs. Terrice said firmly. "For breakfast we have fruit and toast and sometimes an omelet. Luncheon is just salads and cold cuts. With dinner you must take a little more care. Mr. Terrice is fond of fowl, and it must be cooked right. How are you with sauces?"

"I'm able to make all of the standard sorts," Miss Rachel said, taking care not to sound too eager.

"I have the recipes for his favorites, anyway," Mrs. Terrice added. She was busily studying Miss Rachel's physical equipment. "If it weren't for having Shirley I couldn't hire you. But she can do the heavy work and leave you free for cooking. What salary would you expect?"

Miss Rachel unabashedly named the sum she was paying Mrs. Marble, and Mrs. Terrice's eyes flew open.

"I'm—I'm afraid we couldn't quite meet that figure. Would you consider less?"

Miss Rachel considered the food the Terrices were apt to have to eat and said she might. Mrs. Terrice smiled and named a figure, and they bargained pleasantly for a while, and finally it was settled.

"And your references?" Mrs. Terrice asked.

Miss Rachel, without the slightest hesitation, produced the forgery she had composed in the lobby of the St. Regis Arms, and Mrs. Terrice read it hastily and returned it to her.

"That seems to be in order. Now, about uniforms. Do you have your own?"

"Not any new ones."

"They needn't be new. If you are willing to start work today I could let you have some aprons which fit our last cook. She was a large woman—a foreign type. . . ." A shadow of a frown passed over Mrs. Terrice's delicate forehead. "They'll be large for you, but they might do for the day. Do you think you could fix us lunch?"

The Terrices, Miss Rachel thought, must be getting hungry. "I think I might." She let Mrs. Terrice take her on a tour of the kitchen.

It was a large kitchen, tiled profusely in pale blue, well equipped, electrically with refrigerator, range, mixers, and other devices, but the store of food was small and the canned goods which Mrs. Terrice displayed were of an inferior grade.

"Rationing," Mrs. Terrice offered lightly, closing the door of the cupboard on two cans of peas, one of beets, and a jar of pressed chicken. "You won't have to use many canned goods, anyway, since we have a garden. There are six of us, by the way. Myself and my husband, and the children, and two"—she hesitated, smiling a little—"two orphans out of the storm," she finished, with an air of having made a small joke.

Miss Rachel smiled back as though she knew it was expected of her.

"I'll leave you, then," Mrs. Terrice concluded. Plainly she was glad to turn the kitchen and all its works over to someone, even to a little old lady with white hair. "If you need anything Shirley can help you. I'll send her in right away."

She went out, leaving a breath of jasmine sachet in the air, and Miss Rachel decided that it was as good a time as any to discover how an electric range was operated. She was still experimenting when Shirley slid in through the door.

Miss Rachel took a quick peep into the pantry through which Shirley had entered, and out of the back door which let upon a porch and gave a view of lawns and garages. "Now, my dear. I want you to take me upstairs and show me where those bullets were kept. The blanks, I mean, that you brought to Mrs. Terrice."

Shirley looked at her incredulously. "But the police took them last night. And how did you happen to know about them?"

"The newspapers were full of details about the murder. And I had already guessed that the police had taken away the shells. All that I want to see is the lay of the land, so to speak. The places the murderer must have gone hunting for them."

Shirley stood there, young and perplexed, rubbing one temple with the tips of her fingers.

"Didn't Pete tell you anything about meeting me here last night?" Miss Rachel asked suddenly.

Shirley shook her head. "No. Were you?"

"Never mind. How do we get upstairs?" Miss Rachel pushed at her with a recipe book she had picked up off the stove. "I have a room somewhere, don't I? Go tell your aunt I want to see it."

Shirley went away and returned in a moment, looking more puzzled than ever. "She asked if you'd mind sharing my room for just tonight. She wants to clean the cook's room before you use it."

"That's very thoughtful of her," Miss Rachel commented. "Is it the usual thing to clean the cook's room for her?"

"I suppose she likes you," Shirley said innocently. "She didn't do it for the others."

They went up by way of a back stairs which seemed to occupy the space between the pantry and dining room. In the second-floor hall was Pete, using a vacuum cleaner on the carpet. He looked at Miss Rachel and winked dryly. By daylight he was a little huskier, a little younger, than he had been under the moon, but the mocking look was the same.

Shirley smiled at him before she turned to climb the second flight, a brief smile with worry behind it, and she said to Miss Rachel: "He's been swell."

The third floor looked narrower and indefinably shabbier; there was a place in the wall where the plaster had cracked and had never been mended, and Miss Rachel suspected that the carpeting had graced the second-floor hall before it had developed worn spots.

"My room is up here, and Pete's, and Thaw's, and the cook's." Shirley giggled suddenly. "You aren't a bit like a cook, Miss Murdock. I can't imagine you in there." She motioned toward the first door to the right. "She used to snore so, and there was always a smell of garlic about her. I used to think she wore the stuff."

A memory stirred somewhere in the back of Miss Rachel's thought and died away as she went on listening to Shirley's chatter. Garlic . . . the wearing of garlic . . . Didn't it vaguely remind her of something Shirley had said in the booth at the Tea Pot?

Shirley opened the door of her own room. "Here's where I found the blanks finally. In my dresser. Why are you looking at me? Is anything wrong?"

"No. Nothing," Miss Rachel said, going in to examine the stuffed drawers of the dresser. But the half-awake thing in her mind refused to go away.

It was near midnight when she sat up in the dark on Shirley's lumpy bed and felt her heart thud in the beginnings of an utterly ridiculous fear. She had, in the deeps of sleep, remembered what the superstition was about wearing garlic. Garlic was the old middle-Europe charm against things of the night.

Against werewolves, for instance.

8

BUT IN the sunny warmth of the kitchen the next morning, with Shirley bent pink-cheeked over the toaster and the percolator bubbling on the stove, the chill fear of midnight seemed laughable. The cook had been a superstition-ridden peasant from some Balkan dot on the map and probably looked for Dracula on every street corner.

"When the cook left—" she began.

Shirley interrupted at once, breaking off her thought. "The police are furious about her going. Lieutenant Mayhew raised the roof. He wanted her new address, only of course no one knew it."

"I suppose he'll ask for her whereabouts through the newspapers."

"Speaking of newspapers—Uncle John hates them, and he's frozen every reporter who's showed his nose here. I wish you could have seen them." She bent suddenly back to work. "Here comes Thaw."

Thaw Terrice looked pale; the square chin was set and the triangular scar on it stood out like a sharp imprint made with a tool. His eyes, under their heavy brows, settled on Shirley. He said with a touch of awkwardness, "Good morning."

"Good morning," Miss Rachel answered, watching him from across the mixer into which she was breaking eggs for an omelet.

He seemed to take in suddenly the tiny figure inside the wrappings of the cook's huge apron. "Can't I help? Pour the coffee, perhaps?"

"You might," Miss Rachel agreed.

"I'll pour it," Shirley said suddenly, leaving the toast. "I know who wants cream and who doesn't, and all that."

"So do I." A hint of stubbornness had come out on the square chin. "And since I had the idea first, I think the job's mine. Isn't it, Mrs.—Mrs.—" He was looking at Miss Rachel.

"Miss Murd," Miss Rachel supplied, having assumed the easiest alias possible so that she could remember to answer to it. "And I think I'll pour the coffee, if you don't mind."

She took the handle of the pot from under his big hand and went off with it to the dining room. She wanted to see the Terrices this morning, since in avoiding Mayhew she had missed a great deal of what had happened. She wished also to learn what the police had been doing.

The dining room wore a slight air of gloom, though the windows had been thrown open and the sunlight and a faint odor of stock were drifting through them. Mr. Terrice was experimenting with the cantaloupe which Shirley had already served; Mrs. Terrice was writing what looked to be a shopping list, and Lee was looking bored and gorgeous at the far end of the table.

"I can't believe you've always been a cook," she yawned as Miss Rachel stood beside her to pour the coffee. "You're much too nice and you don't smell like a kitchen. I think you've been a lady in waiting somewhere and the fairies changed you to a cook, and in the middle of the night you'll ride away in a pumpkin."

"Lee!" Mrs. Terrice chided. "How fanciful you are this morning!"

"It's an aftermath of those fantastic yarns the lieutenant told us last night. Ballistics! I'm still laughing!"

"Lee!" It was cautioning this time, and the pencil in Mrs. Terrice's hand shook a trifle and made a ragged little mark on the shopping list. "Let's not go into that at breakfast."

Mr. Terrice had put down the spoon beside his cantaloupe. "I must warn you, Lee, to be more careful in what you say. I thought the lieutenant showed admirable patience in listening to you. Especially since what you had to say was trivial and uninteresting. There wasn't any eyewitness to Addison's death. Your suggestion about canvassing the neighborhood must have bored him beyond words."

"Perhaps," Lee said slyly, "that's why he's out doing it this morning."

Mr. Terrice gave a little start and touched his spoon as if to pick it up, and then instead picked a bit of invisible fluff off the tablecloth and dropped it to the floor.

"You see," Lee went on determinedly, "that if we all have alibis—and we all seemed to have, even to Shirley, who told him something in private that must have satisfied him—and if it was quite impossible for a real bullet to have been substituted for the blank because we didn't have any real bullets, then somebody must have come up from *outside* the house and changed that bullet. You didn't; I didn't; Lydia didn't; Thaw didn't." She tapped with a pink nail on the tablecloth to emphasize her points. "We four were together in the den from the time the gun was loaded until poor old Addison was shot. Shirley was out burying a bird, which seems in some mysterious way to have cleared her of suspicion with the police. Pete was in the basement and didn't come up until the excitement started. So—" She shrugged and brushed at the heavy twist of pale hair on her shoulder. "There just had to be somebody else. Somebody who—who had an interest in Addison somehow. . . ."

A peculiar thing had happened to the three people at the table. During Lee's last sentence Mr. and Mrs. Terrice had grown quite still, and their eyes on Lee had a fixed, mesmerized quality, as though they were trying in some soundless way to force her to stop what she was saying. And Lee, looking back at them, let her voice die.

Then she added frigidly: "*She* couldn't have known about the gun."

Mrs. Terrice stood up suddenly. "I have a headache. Please excuse me. Lee dear, when you're quite through with this discussion you might bring me up a little coffee and toast. I'll be in my room."

She went out, and all that remained of her was a lace handkerchief beside her plate and the odor of jasmine sachet.

"I'm stupid today," Lee said contritely. "I'm sorry I mentioned Mo—"

Mr. Terrice literally sprang out of his chair. "Lee! Are you quite out of your senses?"

He turned abruptly to Miss Rachel. "That will be all for now, thank you. We'll ring if we wish anything more."

"I have an omelet," she offered.

"Not this morning," he said brusquely. "I'm sure we won't need it. Do anything you want with it."

In the kitchen Thaw was standing with his back to the room, looking out at the lawns and the gardens through the glass panel of the door; he made a big rugged shape against the blue polka-dot curtains, and the sun struck red lights in his hair. Shirley was putting a pan on for the omelet.

Miss Rachel said: "Do come into the pantry for a moment, Shirley."

Shirley came away with a look of release. Miss Rachel whispered: "What's wrong with him?"

"I don't know. Sometimes I think he's trying to make friends and just doesn't know how. He's cross now because I won't let him help. I wish he'd go out and eat with the others."

"They aren't eating. There was some sort of situation came up which seemed to ruin Mrs. Terrice's appetite, and Lee burst out with an apology for mentioning someone whose name begins with an *M*."

Shirley turned on her a look of wonder. "I don't know who it could be."

"Someone, too, who had an interest in Addison," Miss Rachel remembered. But Shirley's eyes remained blank. Trying another tack, Miss Rachel said: "Did you tell Lieutenant Mayhew that you were with me while the murder was taking place?"

"Yes. Wasn't that right? He seemed to accept it without any question."

"That accounts for what Lee calls your alibi," Miss Rachel murmured. "Do I dare ask Thaw Terrice who the other member of his family is? Yes, I think I do."

She came back into the kitchen quite briskly and took the omelet out of the mixer and poured it into the skillet. "Isn't there someone missing from your family, Mr. Terrice?" she asked of the silent young man at the door. "I was given to understand there was to be one more of you than there is. Or was that a mistake?"

He turned around slowly; there was a kind of repressed anger in his face. "Someone was kidding you, Miss Murd."

She hummed softly and absently, stirring the omelet. "I guess your mother miscounted."

"My—" He checked himself quickly. "Lydia must have had her mind on something else. She wouldn't have told you that." A sudden look of understanding came into his face. "Oh. Perhaps she unconsciously included Addison."

"Hmmm. No, not the gentleman who died." She skated off on very thin and experimental ice. "A lady. A third lady."

He gave her a measuring stare and then bolted out of the room toward the front of the house.

Miss Rachel looked at Shirley across the stove. "Why did he correct me when I called Mrs. Terrice his mother? Isn't she?"

"I thought that she was."

"Just how much," Miss Rachel asked, "did you know about the family before you joined it?"

"Not a great deal. Uncle John was a stepbrother of Mother's. They never saw much of each other after they were grown. She knew that he was married and had two children, nothing more. I don't think that she liked him very well. She wanted me to go to my father's people when she knew that she must— must die."

The sober and sensitive face had turned away; a little feeling of loneliness crept over Miss Rachel.

She began heaping the omelet into a warmed platter. "If you will locate Pete, I think we might eat this. It seems the family isn't hungry."

When Pete had come and the three of them were at the kitchen table Miss Rachel brought up the subject of the gun.

"Whose was it?" she asked Pete. "How long had it been here?"

"It was an old pistol of Thaw's, rather a big thing he sometimes took on hunting trips. He'd had it for years."

She turned to Shirley. "Who had the idea of pointing it right into Addison's face when it went off?"

"I don't know." Shirley stopped in the act of separating a bite of omelet with her fork; turned dark puzzled eyes on Pete. "I guess it was Lee. Someone said, there in the dark of the entry, that it had better go off in his face to have any effect because he was always so—so stupid when he was drunk. And so Thaw fixed it that way."

"Thaw seems to have disliked his uncle intensely. Was there any cause, outside of Addison's drinking?"

"Addison had a knack of getting Thaw's temper up," Shirley said. "It was a mean habit, because Thaw's injuries still hurt him sometimes, and I think that's when he gets snappish and his temper wears thin. Those were the times that Addison liked to bring up old arguments—or fresh ones—and have Thaw jump in and get furious."

"I am beginning to understand how Addison's departure might have been welcomed by almost anybody," Miss Rachel meditated. "What about Lee? How did she and Addison get along?"

Pete said dryly: "Her highness was no end embarrassed by the brute." He made it, somehow, sound like Lee. "The lout actually descended one day upon a sorority party Lee was giving on the back lawn. He did a three-point landing in the punch bowl. It seems he mistook it for a pool."

Shirley was blushing. "Oh, he was dreadfully drunk that day. Last week. It seems a year ago."

"So that, all around, he was strictly undesirable, and the wish to remove him must have been overpowering at times. Still," Miss Rachel wondered, "why didn't they simply ask him to leave?"

"I think the answer to that is the money Addison had," Pete replied. "As long as I've been here I've heard hints from Aunt Lydia about the mistake her parents had made in leaving everything to Addison. It must have been quite a fortune when he first got hold of it. Aunt Lydia more than hinted that part of it was rightly hers. I guess she couldn't risk an open break with Addison by making him get out; she figured she'd lose everything that way."

"Did the man have any other relatives?"

Pete frowned into the cup which had held his coffee. "I could never rightly get the straight of that. I think there was someone, once, and that she died or disappeared. There were three of them in the beginning. I know that much from something Aunt Lydia let drop and which almost caused Uncle John to have fits. What the mystery Was I never could figure. Maybe it's a scandal, something they want to keep quiet."

"Why doesn't Thaw call Lydia 'Mother'? Or Lee, either, for that matter?" Miss Rachel asked, remembering former conversations.

"I don't know." He looked at her blankly. "When I first came I thought it was because Aunt Lydia prides herself on looking so young and that the term 'Mother' might sound old to her. I haven't given it a thought for years."

Miss Rachel sipped her coffee and continued to look thoughtful, and the conversation died.

When the dishes were cleared Miss Rachel slipped upstairs and made preparations to leave. Shirley came in as she was putting on her hat and stood behind her, a slight timid figure in the green wriggly depths of the mirror.

"I have to go out for a while," Miss Rachel told her, giving a final pat to the white hair. "And you must cover up somehow and keep the rest of them from knowing. You might put some lettuce in the refrigerator to crisp for lunch, too, and see what the garden is producing in the way of carrots and cucumbers."

Shirley sat down on the edge of the bed. "Uncle John sent Lee in to say he wants to see me in about a half-hour in the den. It surprised me. He's never been so formal."

"Don't do a thing he tells you until I get back." The very memory of Mr. Terrice's smooth purpose with Shirley the evening before made Miss Rachel yearn to stick him with her longest hatpin. "And don't let him badger you about having a bullet in your hand when he met you in the hall. Remind him that the whole idea belonged to someone else and that you were just the innocent bystander."

"How did you know?" cried Shirley, round-eyed.

"I'm seventy years old," Miss Rachel said, as though that explained everything. "Now keep your wits about you and don't be putty in his hands. Speak up in your own defense."

"Suppose it's the lieutenant?" Shirley gasped. "Suppose he's there with Uncle John?"

"Why should he be?"

"He's found an eyewitness, you know. Oh, you didn't, of course. Well, Lee says that Mrs. Brenn across the street is sure she saw the murderer. He was all black and he flapped. Wings, sort of."

"Amazing!" cried Miss Rachel, putting on her gloves.

She puzzled over the strange hallucinations of Mrs. Brenn all the way to her own house on Sutter Street, and only on her own front porch did she remember Jennifer's black cape.

Mrs. Marble, answering the bell, was bleak. "I don't know as I want to stay, Miss Rachel, even with the raise. It's lonely here in this big house without a soul to speak to. The cat won't eat a bite, and there's queer noises after dark, and I keep thinking about the airplane factories with all their lights on."

"Where is Jennifer?" Miss Rachel asked, going over the mail on the hall table.

"I wouldn't know, miss." A slight wait to give her news good timing; Mrs. Marble was an artist at gossip. "She's gone, bag and baggage, like a thief in the night. She burned a book or something in the fire and then lit out. She left a message for you, miss."

Miss Rachel put down the assortment of letters. "What was it?"

"She said that it was evil stuff you were meddling in and that you'd do best to leave it alone," Mrs. Marble said darkly. "And so I think, miss, I'd just better go away too."

9

Miss Rachel, sitting at her desk in the living room and hearing the rummaging of Mrs. Marble in the floor above, felt very lonely indeed. She sensed the combined displeasures of Lieutenant Mayhew, Jennifer, and Mrs. Marble, and the only restraint to keep her from tearing up her notes about Shirley Grant was the thought of how dull life had been before she had begun dabbling in crime. Knitting and animal welfare weren't in it for excitement when compared with climbing in windows and getting a job on forged references.

She sighed and stacked the notes into a neat sheaf and went out into the hall to the telephone.

Mr. Salter—still dry and somewhat sad even on the phone—had decided that the bird had died from a dose of paint thinner. Paint thinner would give the proper combination of chemicals of which the little bird had been full.

"Would a bird drink such stuff?" Miss Rachel wondered.

Mr. Salter thought that it wouldn't have, that the thinner had been given by means of something like a syringe or an eye dropper. Had Miss Rachel happened to read in the papers, a month or so ago, of the drunken man who had dosed himself similarly, though not meaning to?

"I hadn't read about it, no," Miss Rachel answered. "Narrow squeak with that fellow. He's still in the hospital,"

Mr. Salter informed her. "Guess he'll have a closer look at his bottle next time. Might almost think someone had gotten the idea for your little bird from that case, wouldn't you?"

Miss Rachel said it was possible. "I'll do a little detective work at home." She was almost ready to hang up the receiver.

"Wait a minute," said Mr. Salter. "I want to talk to you about that handkerchief. The one you left with the bird."

Miss Rachel's mind flew back to Shirley, sitting grieving with the dead bird wrapped in a square of cotton. "What about it?"

"Very peculiar thing wrong with it," Mr. Salter went on in his dry tone. "The cloth is full of particles of gunpowder. Not burned powder. The fresh kind you'd get out of a bullet."

He waited as if to get some reaction, but Miss Rachel was far too busy with a confusion of thoughts, main among which was the memory that Addison Brill was supposed to have been murdered with a blank shell that had turned out to be real.

"I see," she managed at last.

"What's going on out at your place?" he asked. "Are you sure that everything's all right? No strangers living with you, or anything like that?"

"Oh no. No one like that."

"Lots of folks are taking in defense workers to board," he ruminated.

"We haven't," she said firmly.

The cat had come to the living-room door and stood looking at her. Samantha was hollow and mournful; her green eyes reproached her mistress, and the black silhouette was thin.

"Shall I cremate your bird for you?" Mr. Salter asked. "He won't keep, you know. Not even full of paint thinner."

"Suppose you do that, and thanks. And you might mail the handkerchief back to me in a plain envelope." She gave Mr. Salter her address and heard him writing it with a dry whisper of a pen.

"How's Mayhew these days?" Mr. Salter asked. "I hear he's giving the ballistics boys some work. Tell him to stop in and see me sometime."

Miss Rachel went cold all over at the idea of asking the next question, but she asked it. "What is the ballistics angle on this murder out here? The Brill man. You know."

"The Brill case? So far as I've heard, it's a straight case of finding the weapon right off. Wasn't there some business of the trigger being tied to a doorknob?"

"I believe so. And thank you so much. Do bring Mrs. Salter to tea someday."

A totally unsuspicious Mr. Salter promised to bring his wife to Miss Rachel's for tea, and the conversation closed with mutual thanks.

Miss Rachel sat in the hall for a moment after she had hung up the receiver, adding penciled lines to the notes she had made on the evening of the crime. She was frowning over the memory of Mr. Salter's reference to a drunken man's mistake with a bottle when Mrs. Marble came downstairs with a suitcase.

"If it's all right with you, Miss Rachel—seeing you've sort of moved away somewhere else anyway—I'd like to go now instead of giving notice. My niece thinks I can get into a riveting class, and they're having interviews this morning. I—I don't hardly know how to say good-by. We've been good friends."

Mrs. Marble had turned away to stare fiercely off into the living room. Miss Rachel left her chair. "Good friends never really say good-by," she said. "And so let's don't, either. We'll see each other again soon. Let me know all about the riveting class, will you? I hope that you'll like it very much."

Mrs. Marble's plain workaday face melted with remorse. "If you really do need me to stay—if there's no one else you can get—"

"We live in perilous times," Miss Rachel said quietly, "and it's so much better for all of us that we have women like you who aren't afraid of tackling a man's job. No, I won't ask you to stay. If Jennifer and I can't do our own house-work we're very poor things indeed. I'm wishing you good luck." She held out a small hand to take Mrs. Marble's big one.

"Take care of yourself," Mrs. Marble muttered huskily. "And don't say I didn't warn you."

She walked away with a firm tread, and the open door showed the sunny street and then drew closed. Miss Rachel, feeling a little lost, went back to the desk in the other room. The cat followed her, a lean reproachful shadow, and when the notes were straight and had been checked and put away Miss Rachel went to the kitchen to feed her.

"I can't leave you alone," she said to the black shape bent above a saucer of fish. "And I couldn't possibly take you with me to the Terrices'. Or could I?"

The result of considerable mental debate on Miss Rachel's part was that when she left her house on Sutter Street the cat was following. Samantha scuttled through hedges and across lawns and lay in wait with green eyes shining wherever shrubs bordered the sidewalk; she thought that she had fooled her mistress, and Miss Rachel was amused by it. But on the Terrice back lawn, peeling an orange, stood Lee, slim in blue blouse and nubbly-textured slacks, and when she saw the cat she pointed in distaste.

"Is it yours? No, it couldn't be. The thing got into the den the night Addison was killed." Her eyebrows, level and fine and almost invisibly dyed a delicate brown, drew together above eyes grown suddenly frosty. "How does it happen that the cat's following you now?"

Miss Rachel looked behind her in pleased surprise. "Well, can you imagine! Is it here? I petted it up the street a way. I think it's lost." She bent down with a look of fatuous affection. "Animals always love me so! Dear little kitty, do you need a home?"

"If it does," Lee said, "it's come to the wrong house. Mother can't abide cats. Dogs, either."

"I'm sure she wouldn't mind if I took the kitty in for a few days until I find it a home," said Miss Rachel, whose mind was made up on this point anyway. "I adore animals. I always have. Will you ask her for me if it might stay?"

Lee shrugged, expressive of disinterest, and walked into the kitchen. Miss Rachel, coming in after with the cat in her arms, found Shirley at the sink keeping a bent head above a bowl of lettuce. There was instantly in the room an air of anger and conflict.

"Are you going to do what Dad asked you to do?" Lee said to Shirley.

Shirley shook her head, and the dark hair swung across her neck and touched the corner of a rebellious mouth. She gave Miss Rachel a brief glance from eyes in which tears stood. "I don't know yet. I'll see about it."

"He wasn't asking much," Lee said as though the matter held small importance, "considering what we've done for you." She walked through the door into the pantry.

Shirley dropped the knife she had been using to trim the lettuce and dabbed at her eyes with the edge of her apron. "What has he done that I should give up the last little thing I own?" she asked Miss Rachel. "The shares in Penny Novelties that Mother's uncle Herbert left her?"

Miss Rachel put the cat down. "And just what is Penny Novelties, my dear?"

"A little company that Mother's uncle started. He invented a funny little toy years ago and couldn't find anyone to put it out and so started his own firm and sank all his money in it. The company barely made expenses. It was a hobby more than a business venture. There's still a factory, I think, a little factory that made metal toys before the war. I don't know what it's doing now."

"But you own stock in it, and your uncle wants this stock. Is that right?" Miss Rachel asked, offering Shirley a handkerchief.

Shirley blew fiercely into the handkerchief. "He says that I should help at least that much. He doesn't ask it as a gift but as a loan—something to borrow money on. I don't see why he wants it. I never knew the stock was worth anything."

"Don't give it to him," Miss Rachel said instantly. "Meanwhile, I'll drop my banker a note and see what he thinks of your stock, and until we have a reply, sit tight. Tell your uncle that you have to have time to think." She hurried through the pantry to the back stairs, heard the cat bound after her in the semi-dark of the stair well. In Shirley's room she scribbled a hasty note on

Shirley's writing paper and sealed it and took a stamp from her purse.

She was conscious suddenly that the cat had not followed her inside and took a quick peep into the hall. Samantha was standing and looking at the door of the cook's room, switching her tail and refusing to come even when Miss Rachel called.

Miss Rachel crossed the hall and knelt down with a rustle of petticoats and put her eye to the keyhole. She saw dimly the metallic shine of the key in its place, and there seemed to be, too, a faint movement from inside the room. Quite silently she turned the knob and learned that the room was locked.

She pressed her ear to the cool varnished panel, and after some moments she caught a sliding noise, a ghost of sound as though a drawer were being shut.

A breath of cool air stole out from under the door to touch her ankles, but there was no further sound. The matter of the note was pressing; Shirley must be protected in whatever scheme her uncle had hatched. With considerable reluctance Miss Rachel gave up her vigil on the cook's room and went back downstairs to the kitchen.

Pete was here now, oiling the mixer and making some adjustment to its motor. He raised a wise eyebrow at Miss Rachel as she went through. Shirley, on the back porch, was putting the lettuce scraps into a covered pail.

"They'll be wanting lunch," Miss Rachel told her. "You might see to the table and put out the cold cuts Mrs. Terrice said they liked at noon. And incidentally, take note of anyone who comes down from upstairs."

Shirley nodded in obedience.

"About the handkerchief you brought me wrapped around your bird," Miss Rachel added, determined to clear up this point while she thought of it. "I'm anxious to know where you got it and how."

Shirley put the pail cover carefully into place and stood holding the plate and looking at Miss Rachel blankly. "Was it a handkerchief?"

"A man's, yes."

"I didn't even remember what it was. I knew it was white and that it—it was just there when I needed something to wrap my bird in."

"You said that Pete came to help you with your bird. Did he give you his handkerchief?"

The sensitive face clouded. "I don't think that he did. But I can't be sure. I found that handkerchief after he had been there in my room."

Miss Rachel walked away feeling a little exasperated. The girl had a timid way of being unsure, of seeming afraid to answer questions with a definite statement. Miss Rachel had repressed an urge to shake her, to shake out a positive yes or no in regard to Pete's ownership of the handkerchief. The handkerchief had had particles of gunpowder in it. Someone had used it, obviously, in some experiment with a bullet— successfully, perhaps, with the blank that had killed Addison Brill.

Walking rapidly along the path that cut across the rear yard and let out upon an alley which Miss Rachel knew to be a short cut to a mailbox, she made the error of looking behind her for the cat. This was an old habit born of Samantha's kittenish way of scurrying after her. Miss Rachel rounded the corner of the garage with her head turned and ran abruptly into the figure of a woman who was standing there.

In the confusion of nearly falling, of clutching at the stucco wall of the garage, and of seeing the woman similarly off guard and discomposed, Miss Rachel took in a scattering of details: the woman's cheap coat fallen open and showing the faded lining, the fallen hat of red straw and ribbon, the hands—worn and roughened hands—that caught for a moment at her own.

Then, regaining her balance, she saw a further and amazing thing. The woman now flattened against the garage as though afraid someone in the house might see her was strangely like Mrs. Terrice. She was, rather, the scrubwoman version of Mrs. Terrice's frail and beautiful forty.

She was thin, but it was not a youthful thinness; it was a worn, sinewy drying up that spoke of poverty and hard knocks. Her hair had a lusterless look, as though it had been improperly washed in too many dirty washbasins and had never seen a curler between times. Her face wore a scattering of freckles across its unhealthy pallor. For a moment, in the shock of being run into by Miss Rachel, her mouth shook in an expression of terror strangely like a child's.

Then she drew away, straightening the sleazy coat and retrieving the red hat from its place upon the lawn. She turned a sullen look on Miss Rachel, and at the same moment, from someplace beyond the shrubbery, the biggest dog Miss Rachel had ever seen slid into view.

He was a great Dane, big of bone and quizzical of eye, and he looked Miss Rachel over as though in prospect of a meal.

"Come, Bucko," the woman said. She began to walk away toward the alley entrance.

"But wait!" cried Miss Rachel, and stopped. What did you say to a duplicate of the woman who had hired you, a strange, bitter caricature of Mrs. Terrice's pink loveliness, a mockery done in shabby clothes as obviously hand-me-down as Shirley's?

"Who are you?" Miss Rachel got out. But only the dog looked back.

10

AFTER SHE had mailed the letter Miss Rachel went back to the Terrice home, but she took in the wide lawns, the walks dappled with shade, and the long graceful lines of the big house with a new eye. There was so much more here, she saw, than a family tired of its alcoholic and abusive member. There was a deep, a chasm in the surface of respectable poise into which she had peered, and none of the Terrices or their possessions could look the same to her.

There was, incredibly, that skulking counterpart of Mrs. Terrice, the shabby duplicate with reddened hands and a trembling mouth, who walked with a great Dane dog in the shadows of the Terrice back yard and slid away when she was asked her name.

And there was—more ominously now—some secret regarding the cook's room. Miss Rachel made up her mind to find out what it was.

She worked for the next half-hour in the kitchen with Shirley. There were carrots to shred, lettuce and tomatoes and cucumbers to chop, a trick of Mrs. Marble's with salad dressing to duplicate. At twelve-thirty Miss Rachel sent in a tray containing the salad with a bowl of dressing to which had been added, with a base of mayonnaise, some chopped chives and pimiento, a breath of garlic, sour cream, and a spoonful of Italian cheese.

She waited, wondering if she had done it correctly, until Shirley came back to say that Mrs. Terrice was enthusiastic about the salad.

"She would be," Miss Rachel murmured. The ghost of the shabby woman wandered across her thought. "What a beefsteak wouldn't do in that direction," she added absently.

"She's afraid, you know," Shirley said, answering the last. "She's afraid she won't stay slim and young."

"So I had gathered. Why?" Setting a place for herself and for Shirley, she puzzled over it. "Why such a determined stand against the forties? Such an uncomfortable time she must have of it. One might think she had some horrible example in mind."

"Addison, perhaps. He'd let himself go dreadfully. He didn't keep himself neat any more, and there was a sort of flabby look to him. As if—Uncle John said—all of his muscles were slowly dissolving in alcohol."

"Speaking of embalming," Miss Rachel said surprisingly, "just what are they doing about Addison's remains?"

"There's to be a funeral tomorrow. I don't know just what time. I—I don't like the idea of going."

"Don't go then," Miss Rachel said briskly. She added a third plate for Pete, who was coming in through the back door. "By the way—while I was gone, who came down from the upper floors?"

"I saw Mrs. Terrice on the stairs. The front stairs, of course. She was talking to Thaw, and I don't know which of them had come down or gone up. They were just there together."

"Hmmmmm." Miss Rachel dished up salad and cold cuts for the three of them, and during the remainder of lunch she seemed very thoughtful. Once when Pete offered her the bread she looked through him as though he weren't there, and to a question from Shirley about giving the cat a saucer of milk she said obscurely: "Perhaps there's some connection."

Afterward, when Pete and Shirley had settled to washing up the dishes, Miss Rachel went off into the front part of the house to find Mrs. Terrice. On the way she took in the details of a little music room she hadn't seen before, where a grand piano sat in lonely splendor, and discovered the whereabouts of the front stairs. The stairs rose from a recess off the living room, behind a screen of gilded ironwork. The carpet on them was soft and deep, and in going up a little way Miss Rachel was able to hear a radio playing softly in some room on the second floor and a voice—Mr. Terrice's smooth one—saying firmly: "The lieutenant wants our cook back. I wonder what he thinks she knows?"

And Lee's reply, from somewhere further in the hall: "He's no doubt going to add her werewolf to his collection, along with the flapping murderer. You might put him wise to the *Rue Morgue*, Dad. He hasn't thought of a gorilla."

Mr. Terrice laughed in a brisk tone that was somehow as expressionless as the eyes behind his shining glasses.

Miss Rachel stole back to the lower floor and studied the living room. It came over her gradually that the pastel colors, the delicate and graceful furnishings, were a frame for Mrs. Terrice and that she must have had the choice in decorating this room. The den was older, more nondescript; the music room was all but empty, the dining room austere, like Mr. Terrice. Here was, somehow, an atmosphere as carefully fragile as Mrs. Terrice's jasmine sachet.

Miss Rachel, slipping through to the door of the den in the small recess leading to it from the living room, saw some quick and momentary movement through a crack of light and, peeping in, she found her eyes held by those of Mrs. Terrice, who stood looking at her from a spot near the mantel.

Mrs. Terrice was cool in a hostess gown of ice-blue net. She frowned a little at Miss Rachel's peering eye, implying that cooks who wandered about peeping in upon the household were somewhat on the undesirable side. "What is it, Miss Murd? Are you looking for me?"

"I'm wondering about my room," Miss Rachel said, coming in. "It was understood, wasn't it, that I was to have the cook's room today?"

Mrs. Terrice took her eyes off Miss Rachel to inspect a fuchsia fingernail. "Was it? I hadn't really remembered. Are you so very uncomfortable in with Shirley?"

"I thought the position included the use of a private room," Miss Rachel said, remembering Mrs. Marble's account of arguments with previous employers on this point, evidently a sore one with servants. "And a private bed. It's hard to rest properly with someone else."

Mrs. Terrice hesitated. "I had wanted to make sure the room was cleaned before you moved in. I'm not sure how Mrs. Lodev kept it. However, since you think the matter important, I'll look up the key. Come back later, will you?"

Miss Rachel heard the door open behind her and looked back. Thaw Terrice had just come in. He was carrying a brief case in one hand and a portable typewriter in the other. There was an expression of tiredness and impatience about him; perhaps, Miss Rachel thought, in the set of the square chin with its triangular small scar. He said to Mrs. Terrice: "May I use this room for a while, Lydia? Lee drives me nuts with her chatter upstairs. If I'm going to finish this course in drafting I've got to work sometime."

He walked to the desk without waiting for her answer and was taking the typewriter out of its case when she spoke.

"I would like to write a letter or two, Thaw. Do you mind?"

He stopped with his hands on the machine. "I do mind, Lydia. I've a job to do. It's a driveling thing compared to getting out in the muck of a South Seas island and handing it to the Japs, but it's the best I'm able to manage and I'm damned if I'm going to wait on your letters. Who are they for, anyway? No one worth blowing to hell, I'll bet."

Lydia shrank at the brutality of his words. "Really, Thaw. Must you be this way?"

Unrelenting, he had drawn up the chair and was jabbing paper into the machine. "If it's answering those ridiculous notes of sympathy that've poured in on you about Addison, forget it. He wasn't worth the scratch of a pen."

Lydia stiffened; the lines about her mouth grew deep, and she took on a sudden appearance of being older. "He was my brother. I'll ask you to remember that."

"He was my uncle, and he had all the qualities of a second-grade skunk," Thaw flung out.

"If you persist in saying things like that," Lydia pointed out angrily, "the police are going to draw some very unfortunate conclusions."

He stopped rolling the paper through and gave her a steady look. "I know exactly what you mean. The gun that killed him was mine. The blanks were mine, left from that silly play Lee dragged me into a year ago. My hand arranged the gun so that it would fire directly into his face." Thaw took a breath, and the scar on his chin twitched with a nervous tic. "Why I haven't been arrested I don't know. The only reason I can think of is that they're waiting to find a motive."

Mrs. Terrice seemed suddenly to take in the fact that Miss Rachel was still standing there. She made a brief imperious gesture toward the door. "Leave us, please, Miss Murd. I'll talk to you later about your room."

Thaw Terrice seemed to give Miss Rachel a quick attentive stare as she withdrew. Was it, Miss Rachel wondered, because he, too, had suddenly realized that she was there listening to their quarrel? Or could it have been Mrs. Terrice's mention of the cook's room which had caused him to turn around and to watch her as she left?

She found a short wide hall in which were doors leading to the dining room, to the serving pantry, and to a closet where wraps were stored. Back again in the kitchen, she found it empty except for her cat, who stood with raised tail and slitted eyes, staring toward the rear entry, where the door was now opened for coolness, leaving only the screen.

A quick glance at the out-of-doors showed the tail and rear legs of a great Dane disappearing into the shadow of a hydrangea bush.

And then a firm tread and a big figure that filled the doorway and looked in.

Miss Rachel darted back into the pantry. The big man was Mayhew, an unmistakable bulk against the sunny light. She wondered if he had seen her. Had he, by any chance, noticed the disappearing dog or caught a glimpse of his mistress? With a cautious eye at a keyhole she watched as he surveyed the kitchen and then turned to stare about the yard. She risked opening the door a crack and coaxed her cat through it and hurried upstairs to the second hall.

Here the radio still played in one of the rooms, more softly than ever since all doors were closed.

Up in the gloom of the third floor Miss Rachel went slowly and listened. There was no scrape of sound behind the cook's door. When she put her ear to the panel there was nothing but stillness, and there was, too, no breath of air against her ankles. Some opening in the room which had given ventilation had been closed.

She tried the keyhole again and found it stuffed with a bit of cotton which she promptly pulled out. She had now the view of the corner of a window with a dirty pane and the top of a high iron bedstead. By practically sticking her eye into the opening and craning her neck she could see part of an object which was sitting in the middle of the window sill. It was a small square object with a stripe of red. It looked a little like a miniature candy box. But stretch and peer as she might, Miss Rachel could not quite see all of it. She went to work, eventually, on the lock with hairpins.

By the time she had bent beyond repair some six or seven of these irreplaceable utensils Miss Rachel gave up. She took her cat and went to sit in Shirley's room until Shirley should come and could find out if Mayhew was still around.

Shirley's battered clock ticked off a half-hour before she came, looking radiant, in a hurry to get into her closet and be off again. "Lee's given me something, Miss Murdock! Oh, it's lovely! That red robe she wears sometime at breakfast. Perhaps you haven't seen it, though. Silk chenille with white fur pockets, and epaulets made out of tiny white tails, and a big clip at the throat like a latch—"

"I haven't seen it, but it sounds gorgeous. Why is she giving it to you?"

Shirley flung her a quizzical look. "I don't know. Perhaps she's tired of it. I'm to bring some hangers for her—that's why I came here first. I've loads, you see."

Shirley's closet was indeed a veritable storehouse of extra hangers. Miss Rachel watched while the girl gathered up a half dozen or so, tested them with the tips of her fingers for snags and irregularities, and made again for the door.

Miss Rachel stood up to block her way.

"I believe I'll go with you. I'd like to see Lee's room."

There was a moment before Shirley understood. "Oh, of course. Do you think there might be evidence in it?"

"One never knows. I'd like to see inside, at any rate."

"Have you—any suspicion about who killed my bird?"

Miss Rachel looked at her thoughtfully. "I've begun to get ideas. Nothing definite yet, however."

"It seems queer," Shirley said on the way out, "to be worrying about me when such important things have happened. Addison getting killed. A murderer who flapped. The cook frightened away by what she thought was a werewolf."

"Hmmm. I think your bird has his place in it somewhere," Miss Rachel murmured. She followed Shirley down into the second floor, where a quick reconnaissance showed no sign of Mayhew. Shirley was opening a near door, and the radio music swelled out into the hall.

Miss Rachel's first impression of Lee's room was that it had been whipped up by a whole convention of decorators. Nothing so deliberately streamlined and *soigné* could have existed otherwise. A wide bed with a padded headpiece stood across the room; the spread of quilted cream-colored satin taped with burgundy had its echo in the window draperies and in the skirt of the dressing table. A radio in bleached oak stood with a blue hassock in a corner. Two little book-cases held an assortment of checkerware pottery, miniatures in which the light reflected softly, and a fuzzy rug in aquamarine made a seascape of the floor.

Shirley had gone to a great mirrored panel in the left wall and had pushed it back, and there stood revealed a long row of clothing: suits and coats and dresses, with hats on a shelf above and shoes in a rack below, and one whole section of house coats and negligees in colors from plum to pale pink, like a spectrum done in reds.

Shirley put in a careful hand and took out something shimmering and slim: a long red silky thing with *bouffante* pockets of white fur and a frosting of little tails on either shoulder.

She caught it up to her and put a knee out to press its silky length, and Miss Rachel heard her breath from where she stood by the dressing table.

Miss Rachel turned and looked at the array of Miss Terrice's perfumes and colognes: bottles of all sizes and shapes which crowded there, and, seeing an old favorite—Bluebonnet at ten dollars the bottle—she reached and picked it up.

One whiff of Bluebonnet, when Miss Jennifer let her squander ten dollars to get it, was enough to wrinkle Miss Rachel's little nose in ecstasy, and she had a guilty idea of putting a dab, perhaps, on a handkerchief and tucking it into the suitcase she kept in Shirley's room.

She removed the cap off the cologne and sniffed.

An astonished look came over Miss Rachel; she all but inhaled the contents of the bottle and then she turned rapidly to the others.

Shirley was stroking the rippling silk; she didn't see Miss Rachel's rapid and incredulous foray among Lee Terrice's perfumes. She may have heard the chink of glass, the faint scratch of tops being screwed off and replaced, the rustle of Miss Rachel's petticoats as she moved across in front of the dressing table. If she did hear, she paid no attention.

She and Miss Rachel both jerked to attention, though, when Lee's voice said icily from the door: "Will you leave my room, please? And let the things that I have left alone?"

11

"She didn't like us being in her room," Shirley worried as they hurried to the third floor like a pair of reproved children. "And still—she'd told me to go there for the robe."

Miss Rachel cast a speculative eye on the shimmering stuff in Shirley's arms. "Just how happy was she over giving it to you?"

"I don't know. Perhaps I was too excited to notice." The delicate face with its unsure, sensitive eyes turned toward Miss Rachel. "But would she have offered it unless she wished me to have it?"

"Hmmmm. Do you know whether she had been with her father previously?"

They paused in the third-floor hall, where the old carpet put a musty smell in the air and the long shadows were dun-colored. "I believe she and Uncle John had been in the den. That was after he'd spoken to me about giving him the stock. Lending it, I mean."

"And she came out from speaking with him and asked if you wanted the robe?"

"No." Shirley shook a dark head. "She came into the kitchen and stopped by the sink and asked me if I remembered her red robe with the fur on it, and when I said yes she sort of flung out: 'Well, it's all yours now.' As though it didn't amount to much."

A spark of anger shone in each of Miss Rachel's usually mild blue eyes. "How rude she is! And how silly to think that the gift of the robe will make you turn over your stock to Mr. Terrice."

Shirley paused in the act of opening her door. "Do you mean—do you think there's something more—?" She held the silky stuff away and looked at it with a new glance.

"There is undoubtedly something more," Miss Rachel said. "And you must promise me again that you won't let that stock out of your possession until I hear from my banker."

There was brief tear-shine in Shirley's eyes before she turned quickly to go in. "I promise. I won't let him have it."

When the red robe had been put away they went down to start preparations for dinner. On the sink, newly arrived as though it had flown in, lay a duck. Miss Rachel, wrapping herself in one of the cook's huge aprons, gave it a puzzled stare.

"How do you defeather a duck?" she asked. "Isn't there a secret to it? Or does it have to be a sort of pillow-fight effect?"

They were making tentative gestures toward jerking feathers out when Pete came in with the vegetables from the garden. For a minute he stood watching them with a look as though he were trying not to be amused; then he put down the vegetables and proceeded to give a demonstration.

"The secret of plucking a duck is paraffin," he said, slipping a cake of it into a pan of hot water. When the paraffin had melted he ruffled the hot solution well into the feathers of the duck, let the wax solidify, then took out duck feathers easily by the handfuls.

"Pete knows how to do so many things," Shirley said softly

in admiration, and even after Pete was gone and she and Miss Rachel were busy making dressing she wore a little smile of pleasure.

But Miss Rachel, chopping celery, was frowning. "Since Pete is versatile and young, why does he stay here? The Terrices treat him like a handy man and janitor. They must pay him little or nothing."

"Nothing," Shirley put in. "I don't think he even gets an allowance."

"With such opportunities as there are," Miss Rachel said, remembering Mrs. Marble's class in riveting, "why isn't he out taking advantage of some of them? Or in the Army, since he is of age?"

"The Army rejected him because of a damaged ear. Pete had scarlet fever when he was little, and there were some complications afterward which Mr. Terrice didn't think were important enough to have treated. About the opportunities for work, I don't know." Shaking a bit of thyme into the bowl, Shirley bit a lip in thought. "Sometimes I've hoped he stayed because of me. He's the only one who's been friendly or helpful—except Thaw when he isn't moody, and of course he can't help that. Pete sort of hinted one day that if we had a little money we might go away together."

"How long ago?" Miss Rachel asked sharply.

"A few days." She raised puzzled eyes. "That was the day he found me crying over a wet mop that had somehow gotten upon Lee's white shoes. I guess he saw how I felt, how miserable I was."

Mincing bread crumbs, Miss Rachel studied the bowl rim, and her gaze was thoughtful. When the duck was dressed and the sauce simmering she took Shirley to the corner where the mixers stood—well away from either door—and said quietly: "I want the key to the cook's room. Do you know where it is?"

"The key?" Shirley seemed to take a moment to study out Miss Rachel's meaning. "Do you mean that the cook's room is locked?"

"It is, and I want mightily to unlock it." Miss Rachel stretched her five feet two to peep out of the window over the sink; she was beginning to see Lieutenant Mayhew behind every shadow. "I think I'd like Mr. Terrice's key ring. That should have a master key of some sort on it."

"He does carry quite a few keys," Shirley answered. "But why should he lock the cook's room? Is there something valuable in there?"

"There is something inside which interests someone. How valuable it is I couldn't say. Suppose you run along and see if you can get hold of Mr. Terrice's keys."

Shirley shrank a little. "He wouldn't like that, and I don't see how I could manage anyway."

"Go and have a look at him." Miss Rachel gave her reluctant assistant a little push. "Meanwhile, I'll slip up and be there if you come. I'll have a peep inside while I'm waiting."

"But if it's someone in the family who's locked the room," Shirley worried, "wouldn't that be eavesdropping? Spying's so— so cheap."

"It doesn't hold a candle to murder."

Shirley's eyes grew big in a white face. "M-murder? But you said—about my little bird—"

"No, I didn't," Miss Rachel corrected, having grown a little tired of having constantly to remember that she was here about a bird. "You did. Remember? I just said that I wanted a look at them, at the Terrices. To begin with, I discovered Mr. Terrice

trying to pin the murder of Mr. Brill on you on the very evening it had happened. And you weren't doing very well defend-
ing yourself."

"Oh, that?" Shirley looked blindly about, as though in a fog.
"He says now that it was all a mistake."

"He won't if he sees the police reaching for one of them." She
gave another push. "Get along. Where does he keep his keys?
On him?"

"I haven't any idea."

"Then find out." Miss Rachel stirred the sauce, turned out
the blaze under it, peered in at the duck oozing stuffing, and
made for the back stairs. She found her cat in Shirley's room,
rolling over and over in an excess of mischief, a bit of white fluff
in her paws. For a moment, seeing the gossamer fragment, Miss
Rachel had a horrid fear that Samantha had played tricks on
the white fur of Shirley's robe. Then, extracting the bit from between the black paws and spreading it in her palm, she sat still
for a long while and stared. The thing in her hand was a piece
of feather, and from it—when she put it to her nose—came the
faint dry smell of paraffin.

"Pete!" she whispered, and raised her head and looked about
the room and found no change in it. Shirley's unlovely bed with
its plain white counterpane stood by the windows; the dresser
with the cracked glass was opposite; two lonely-looking chairs
flanked the door. The room was sunny with a late-afternoon
light, and the characterless hand-me-down furniture reminded
her somehow of Shirley's meekness. She got up and began to
search the room in a very frenzy of anger.

There was nothing to be found; no lurking mystery under
the bed or in the closet or added to the crammed contents
of the dresser. Miss Rachel shook out all bedclothes, ran the

blinds down to their full length, investigated the two pictures, Bopeep and Miss Muffet, which must have been shoved off here when some room below had been remodeled from Lee's nursery.

And she found nothing hurtful, nothing new, nothing strange.

Back at the closet, she looked in to where the red robe hung alone in a little space cleared out by pushing the shabby clothes together on the rod, and at sight of the red silky glitter, the big puffed pockets and the epaulets of little tails, she unaccountably stuck out her tongue.

Then, feeling quite cross, she took the cat and went out into the hall and listened. After some minutes she heard stealthy steps coming up; a fearful and white-faced Shirley peeped up from the stair well at her.

"Yes?" whispered Miss Rachel.

There was a ring full of keys of all sorts and sizes clutched in one of Shirley's hands. "He was taking a b-bath," she stammered. "I could hear the shower running between his room and Lydia's, and his wallet and handkerchief and keys were lying on a chest at the foot of his bed. He'll be dreadfully angry. I—I don't know how to get them back to him afterward."

"I'll think of something," Miss Rachel promised. She had taken the keys from Shirley's uncertain fingers and was jabbing one after the other of them at the keyhole. When she had made the rounds twice with all of them she raised and stared at the white face so near her own.

"The right key isn't here. He doesn't have it. Or he doesn't, at least, keep it on his key ring."

Shirley went to the door and bent and put an eye to the little beam of light. "Why do you wish to get inside? Do you think there might be something important there? A clue? A clue about—about Addison?"

Miss Rachel noted thankfully that Shirley at last no longer kept the illusion that she was interested solely in the bird. "I'm wondering about that room. Try to see the window sill. There is a box of some kind sitting there."

Shirley's slight form pressed and wriggled. "The small thing with the red stripe on it? I've seen that somewhere before. I—I can't quite remember where. In Thaw's room when I dusted there? I wonder. . . ."

Miss Rachel sighed in impatience. "We might as well try to get Mr. Terrice's keys back to him. Go down and peep in and I'll follow." She let Shirley precede her down the stairs, waited while the black cat strolled from step to step and rubbed her back against the bars of the railing. By the time she had reached the lower hall and caught sight of Shirley again the girl was hurrying to the front stairway, and every line of her expressed terror and dread. For an instant Miss Rachel felt the contagion of discovery. There was no doubt, from Shirley's actions and from the peculiarity of Mr. Terrice's door being open, that the man had missed his keys.

Then she smoothed the big cook's apron and picked up the cat and walked resolutely toward the door that was ajar.

Mr. Terrice stood just inside it. His small well-proportioned figure was fitted neatly with a plum-colored robe. His brushed hair was sleek, and where it thinned at the top his scalp looked pink and glowing. The glasses regarded Miss Rachel with unusual brightness. His hands held a wallet and an immaculate new handkerchief, and when his gaze settled on the ring of keys in Miss Rachel's fingers he put the other articles slowly into a pocket of the robe.

"You have my keys," he said without expression. "How did you find them?"

"The cat was playing with them on the steps down to the kitchen," she explained. "I didn't know whose they were, but I thought I'd ask you."

He studied the cat with an oblique glance, and there was a little space of silence that Miss Rachel didn't like. "I see," he said at last, and took the keys from her. "I don't understand the animal being here. Are you sure that Mrs. Terrice gave you permission to keep it?"

"Your daughter was going to ask her for me. I haven't had an answer yet."

"You'd better check up on it, then." He had turned back into the room, and Miss Rachel peeped past his shoulder and saw a big ornate mahogany bed, a carved chest, and a dark rug that made the whole room seem gloomy. The place was as spare and as immaculate as Mr. Terrice himself, and as utterly without humor as the eyes behind his shining glasses.

"Thank you for bringing the keys," he added, and Miss Rachel found the door being closed in her face.

She went down into the kitchen, where Shirley was furiously busy with vegetables. "Did he catch you?" Shirley wondered. "I was just about to peek into his room when he opened the door and stood there looking at me. I almost died."

"I told him that the cat had the keys, playing with them." Miss Rachel looked in upon the duck, adjusted the oven, tasted a bit of sauce on the end of a spoon. "I'm going to leave you for a little while and go upstairs. If I can't unlock that room I might at least find out who's using it, and why. Keep Samantha for me, will you? She meows at people sometimes."

"I wish"—Shirley had dropped a carrot—"I wish you wouldn't. It's queer about the room being locked." She put up a hand to push away a tendril of hair; she looked suddenly tired, suddenly older. "I feel as though someone's planning something, using the room in some horrible way to get ready to—kill again."

"You feel that too?" Miss Rachel murmured. "Yes. It's an obvious conclusion."

She went out, with Shirley's eyes following her, and found the second floor deep in silence and the hall of the third floor growing gray with twilight. In Shirley's room the shadows had crept up the left wall so that Bopeep and Miss Muffet made white squares against the dark wall, and the bed and dresser cast triangular shapes along the floor.

She sat down in one of the slatternly chairs beside the door, feeling the old wood creak under her slight weight, and with an ear to the crack she waited. From far away, through Shirley's window, came the cheep of a drowsy bird settling itself and the groan of traffic on a boulevard that led down toward the sea. The tick of Shirley's clock kept pace with the slow darkening of the room; so many ticks to each inch of shadow, so many minutes between daylight and dark, a half-hour to bring chill in at the open window and show street lights beginning to bloom along the streets outside.

The dinner would have to be served; further absence from the kitchen might be suspicious. Miss Rachel rose from the chair, feeling weary and depressed.

She stood facing the wall on which the nursery pictures hung, and something shadowy that had begun to emerge from Miss Muffet held her there, breathless, her heart beginning to thump with fear. A bluish and uncertain shape, a phantom, a thing with ears and black holes of eyes and a jagged reach of fang stared out at her. She felt the dry breath catch in her throat, heard thunderous terror seize her pulse.

In the darkness of Shirley's room a werewolf's face looked down at her and grinned.

12

DETECTIVE LIEUTENANT Stephen Mayhew came away from Mrs. Brenn's house and felt the grateful cool of her garden and sighed. Beyond the pepper tree, a fantasy in lace against a pearl-gray sky, the big and proper homes of Chestnut Street showed a few lighted windows, gave an air of massive settling down before the dark. In the Terrice home almost directly opposite the wide windows of the living room were blank. The small entry with its circular embrasure and its two little niches was in deep shadow. From an upper room, behind windows which Mayhew placed as having been those of the late Mr. Brill, a soft glow shone.

A whole series of remarks in Mrs. Brenn's chattering voice ran through his mind—the woman was able to talk endlessly about almost nothing—but here and there she dropped something of value. The things she had dropped about Mr. Brill were that he had been a drunkard—which Mayhew had gathered—and that the neighborhood disapproved of him and that somewhere he had another sister besides the lovely Mrs. Terrice.

"I've seen her," Mrs. Brenn divulged, "with my own eyes.

And a sorry, shabby thing she is, all bones and red hands and the awfullest clothes. Mr. Brill always acted nice to her, though. One night they stood right in my garden and she cried on his arm. I awoke and thought they might be making love or perhaps getting ready to burgle my house and would have called the police, only about then I recognized Mr. Brill. Big, you know, and with those unpressed clothes. So I just waited and watched and pretty soon I heard him say, 'Look, Sis, it was bad luck and all that, but you can't go on crying about it all your life.'"

"You are positive," Mayhew had answered, "that these were his exact words?"

"Yes, and then she said, 'I suppose if you weren't my brother you wouldn't have put up listening to me all these years, would you?' And he kind of burbled something back at her, something sort of drunk that he meant to be comforting. I guess Mr. Brill had his good points, at that."

"Did you see this other sister in the daylight?"

"Well, not daylight, just. Very, very early one morning, when things were just beginning to get light." Mrs. Brenn made an expressive skyward gesture with a fat hand. "I hadn't slept well and I went out to see how the pansies were doing—snails, you know—and there were this woman and Mr. Brill walking up the street together. Mr. Brill was dreadfully drunk, but the woman wasn't, I don't think, and she was plodding along like a horse, almost, dragging a heavy load. Pulling Mr. Brill along home."

Mayhew had taken out his notebook. "Give me her description, please."

"But I did! I mean she's awfully thin and wears old clothes."

"Color of eyes, hair, height and approximate weight, and so on."

"Oh." Mrs. Brenn's placid eyes grew wide. "I was never very good at that sort of thing. Sinus, you know, keep sniffling and all that. She had a dog."

"A dog?" Mayhew echoed.

"A dreadfully yellow sort of dog."

Remembering the conversation, its ramifications and addenda, the grip he had kept on his patience during Mrs. Brenn's discourses on the breeds of dogs, former dogs she had owned, the way Mr. Sanders next door treated his dog, the ways in which a dog could be housebroken, and a sudden scurry off into the ethics of running a flower show, Mayhew groaned. And the light in the dead Mr. Brill's windows was as the adding of a fleabite to a third-degree burn. It was the bit that made too much.

Mayhew crossed the street and deliberately chose the path to the back door and so presently looked in upon an empty kitchen. He knocked without enthusiasm and, not being answered, stepped inside. From beyond some interconnecting door he could hear a soft clink of glassware and silver. "Dinner," he thought, "is served. I'll run along upstairs just as if I don't know there's a soul in the house. It's highly irregular, but it's fun." For no reason at all he remembered suddenly some of the antics of Miss Rachel.

In the second-floor hall he paused and took in the deep-pile rug and the shaded light. He had seen it before, but he liked looking at it again. When policemen, he promised himself, started making the kind of money stockbrokers made this was the sort of place he would have. He moved along quietly to the front of the house, much as a bear trying to tiptoe, and tried the door of Mr. Brill's room and pushed it open.

There she sat, looking at him in life.

In the first instant of surprise at finding her there Mayhew had nothing to say. It was she, looking at him from across a manicure set, who spoke. She put down a nail file with which she had been trimming the broken and ragged nails; she smoothed the cotton skirt of dun-colored plaid. "You're cops, aren't you? Who let you in here?"

"I'm investigating the death of Mr. Brill," Mayhew said officiously and came in.

"Don't shut the door." She pointed behind him. "You're going right out again."

"You'll have to explain who you are and what you're doing in the dead man's room."

"To you?" She laughed, and the sallow skin wrinkled dryly at the corners of her lips. "Why should I?"

"You'll find that it pays to be helpful." Mayhew cast a look over the room, took in two pieces of obviously new, cheap luggage, a sleazy coat flung on the bed, a red hat with a feather on a chair. "There isn't any point in your not cooperating. Everyone who comes into or leaves the house is investigated. We can do it pleasantly or—otherwise."

Her sullen mouth relaxed. "Oh, all right. Fire away. I haven't got anything to hide. Not any more." Her eyes defied him.

He took out his notebook and a pencil and waited while she uncorked a small red bottle and began painting her nails. "Name?"

"Lissa Brill Terrice. *Mrs.* Terrice, if you're curious." The soft light lent no loveliness to her bent head. Mayhew had never seen so lusterless a mop. "I'm forty-three and free and white. What else?"

"Where do you work?"

She hesitated; the red brush made a tiny blotch on her skin where she hadn't meant it to. "Nowhere. Not any more. I used to do—well—I sort of worked at night. Cleaning."

He wrote: *janitress,* while she watched him. "Now. What caused you to come here and how do you happen to have the name of Terrice?"

"I came because I was invited. Ask Mr. Terrice." She held off a hand to survey it; she must have seen the curious color scheme made by the reddened skin and the too-scarlet nails. She put the hand down quickly as if to conceal the paint. "I'm—I'm a member of the family. That's how I happen to have the name."

"You are Mr. Brill's sister, I believe. That means you must have married into the Terrice family."

"That's right."

He made an impassive bulk between her and the door; her eyes crept up to take in his huge shape, the square inexpressive face with its steel-colored eyes and its stubborn patience. "Are you married now to a member of the Terrice family?"

"No. Divorced."

"From whom?"

"From"—she bit at her lip—"from John. John Terrice."

Mayhew had the impression, somehow, that she enjoyed telling this, that it had been bottled up inside her and she was glad to give it out.

"You are, then," he said, choosing a thought at random, "the mother of Mr. Terrice's two children?"

Her eyes jerked toward him and then stopped; some brief fire died in them. "You'd better ask them that question."

"You think they might not claim you?"

Bitterly: "They might not. Lee might not."

"But Thaw?"

The sullenness came back, and Mayhew saw that it was a mask, a ready mask she had learned to put on to hide other things. "Ask him."

"I've noticed," Mayhew said conversationally, sitting down on a chair near her, "that Thaw never refers to the present Mrs. Terrice as his mother."

She began painting her nails again. "You noticed that?"

"And your dead brother—he was loyal to you too. Wasn't he?"

"I guess so—in his own way. Poor devil."

"Do you know anything about how he died?"

She shrugged, recorked the nail paint, and closed the box of manicure implements. "Just what I read in the papers."

"How long since you'd seen him?"

She paused with the box in her hands and seemed to study the catch. "Quite a while. A week or so. I don't remember."

"You didn't see him the night of his death?"

"No."

"When did you contact the family?"

She looked a question at him. "I mean," Mayhew explained, "how did you happen to know that the family wanted you to come here?"

For a moment there was almost a smile; there was something else, too, in the depths of her eyes. A vindictive happiness, Mayhew thought. "They didn't really want me. I'm here because of Addison's will. My brother left a lot of money and some property and some securities. All of what he left has to be evaluated

and the total divided according to percentages. His will specified that all beneficiaries must be gathered together for the final
settlement. He wasn't taking a chance, you see, that they'd try
to brush me off."

"Who got in touch with you?"

Her glance evaded his. "Mr. Terrice. My former husband."

"Do you mind telling me about your divorce from Mr.
Terrice?"

"Not at all." Again she smoothed the dun-colored skirt,
brushed away a lock of straggling hair in which no light was
reflected. She was, Mayhew thought, pitifully like a child—an
old child—with a small story to recite. "It isn't a long story, nor
a new one. When Mr. Terrice and I had been married four years
my younger sister came to live with us. I had the chil—I had
responsibilities, and I felt tired much of the time, and I guess I
was letting myself go. You know." She flung him a glance. "My
sister was—is—very careful of herself. When she was younger
it was just incredible how pretty she could look. She was like—
like something made out of whipped cream and strawberries."

Mayhew thought: "She still is. And why in hell can't you be
more like her?"

She had found a snag in the dun-colored skirt and was picking at it. "They came to me one day, a sort of muggy day in late
summer, while I was sitting on the terrace fanning myself and
trying to keep the—well, never mind. They came up hand in
hand, and it struck me, before either of them spoke, how well
they looked together. Mr. Terrice had always been neat. He has
a horror of untidiness. And my sister was wearing a soft little
green dress that made her hair seem pure gold. They said they
loved each other." Some convulsive movement seized her throat,
and she looked the other way. "That's all. That's all there was."

For a long moment Mayhew sat silent, and something in the air of the room had become oppressive and distasteful, and the house itself seemed new to him. He looked about the big room, at the bed covered richly with blue silk, at the drapes of some heavy soft stuff that shone where the light touched it, at the deep rug in pale rose, and his square mouth drew in so that there was a white space above and below the lips, and the line of his jaw was hard.

"I'm sorry for something I thought about you," he said unaccountably. "You wouldn't want to be that way."

She turned to look at him, puzzled, and he went on briskly: "Now. Have you any ideas about your brother's murder?"

"Ideas? Of what use would they be to you?"

"I'm not sure," he said frankly. "Suppose you let me judge."

"Well . . ." She had gone back to plucking the snag. "Addison was rich. He left a lot of money. But you know that."

"You spoke about percentages. Can you explain that further?"

"I get half of everything he owned—half of the total, that is—and I have the choice of properties to make up my share." Mayhew was looking at her queerly.

"I know what you're thinking," she said. "You're thinking that I had a motive for killing him. But that crazy stunt with the gun—I wasn't in on that. So get the idea out of your head."

Mayhew mentally filed it, with the added note that Addison's death not only made the first Mrs. Terrice a lady of wealth, but gave her also entry into a family from which she had been cast out. "What else can you tell me about your brother? Anything I might not know?"

"He had a quarrel with someone here on the day before he died."

"Who?"

"Some kid named Pete, some relative of John's he's taken in since I left him."

Mayhew studied her intently. "What did your brother tell you about this quarrel?"

"Just that he had it." She shrugged. "He said he'd got onto something—he didn't say what—and that he jumped Pete about it."

"That's damned vague," Mayhew said.

"He was drunk when he told me, mumbling and threatening to see that things were set right. He didn't explain what Pete had to do with the affair."

"I'll check on it," Mayhew promised under his breath.

"And I don't know anything more." She said it with a sudden effect of regretting everything she had told him, and put out a hand and stroked the silky spread as though its feel were new to her. "I'm going to take a bath and lie down. Do you mind getting out now?"

He rose and thanked her and saw her kick off her shoes before he had quite shut the door behind him.

The hall was still richly carpeted and as softly lighted as before, but Mayhew made no pause to take it in. He strode to the back stairs—the only ones which led up to the third floor—and took them two at a time. He rattled the knob of the cook's door and found it locked and thought of forcing it and then decided to leave the Terrice house intact—the shabby, starved woman below wasn't the house's fault exactly. He went to Shirley's door and looked in.

The room was quite dark, so that the light from the hall made a dim rectangle on the floor and touched the faded bedspread with a band of yellow. "Damned little place," Mayhew said soundlessly, "and what the devil kind of a picture is that?"

On the wall hung a nursery rhyme and another thing—an empty frame through which the pattern of the wallpaper showed in blowzy garlands. Mayhew walked and turned the glass and took it from the wall. "She's found something," he muttered angrily, and put it back.

He was like a bear in the stair well, a big brown-coated bulk with an angry set to his shoulders. "*Miss Murd*," he flung at the dark. "How she must think me a fool!"

13

Miss Rachel was in the dark behind the garage, crouched close to the wall, watching with big eyes while the last crackle of flame consumed a largish piece of stiff paper.

"Burning evidence?" Mayhew asked pleasantly from the oleander bushes, and she jumped.

He came out where she could see him and stood with his hands in his coat pockets. He made a huge bearlike shadow on the garage when the flame rose just before it died, and the toe of one shoe came forward to investigate the ashes. "Looks like a picture of some sort. A kid's picture. Old nursery stuff."

She listened for the note in his voice which would have told her he was guessing and failed to find it. "It had been," she said miserably. "But it had something more now, something quite— quite hideous and cruel."

He stood there impassively; Miss Rachel wondered if he knew how really afraid she was. "There had been a wolf's head painted upon it in luminous paint. Nothing to show by daylight. But in the dark, you see, after the lights were out—she'd have looked up sometime, and there it would have been. The were-wolf."

The last glow faded from the curled ashes with a tiny snap. "And so you thought you'd just put a match to it. You don't like the police," Mayhew said grimly.

"You're dreadfully angry, aren't you?"

Mayhew shrugged. "People have been put into jail for less."

"I suppose so." She felt blushes steal over her. "I suppose you've a perfect right to run me off in the middle of things."

"So that worries you?" He took a step and touched her elbow gently. "Come over here. There's a bench in a cleared space where we should be able to talk out of earshot of everybody. Walk quietly. Someone's come into the kitchen and is looking out."

Crossing the grass beside him, she peeped beyond his brown bulk and saw Thaw's figure in the door; he made a restless move as if to touch the knob and come out, and then swung suddenly around and walked away. The light in the kitchen shone on his dark head, showed rebellious fingers rubbing the scar upon his chin.

"I feel sorry for that boy," Miss Rachel whispered, "even if he does turn out to be the one who killed Addison."

Mayhew's square face looked down at her. "Sympathy for a possible murderer? It isn't like you."

"I know. But Thaw is—a victim, a result of war. His whole viewpoint has been twisted by seeing his friends butchered in battle. He's out of touch with convention, with ordinary rules of conduct. He must, right now, be going through a sort of h-hell."

"Strong language from a lady. Hmmmm. And you suspect, too, that he might have knocked off Addison in the same way he'd swat a fly? Just casually?"

"I don't know." She sat down by Mayhew on the bench and

looked at the dark ring of the horizon and the stars. "He might have. So might any of the others."

"No conclusions yet? What about Miss Grant and her ghostly persecutor?"

"It's not a ghost."

A cricket began a steady chirping from the oleanders and then stopped on a half note as a leaf crackled. Something yellow and long-legged came out to watch them in the dark, and Miss Rachel rose with the beginnings of a shriek.

"You're losing your nerve," Mayhew chided. "Mustn't let it get you. This is only Mrs. Terrice's yellow dog."

He wagged no tail at them but stood quiet and solemn in the fringe of shrubbery by the garage. Miss Rachel sank back upon the seat. "Mrs. Terrice? No, you're wrong. Mrs. Terrice's sister's yellow dog."

"Correction. There were two Mrs. Terrices. The first one made the mistake of bringing home her young sister. Sister had looks, no brats to rub off the polish, no scruples about getting what she wanted. She wanted Mr. Terrice. Mr. Terrice reciprocated. Exit the first Mrs. Terrice, to acquire red hands and old clothes and a great Dane. The great Dane, I judge, simply for something to love. The second Mrs. Terrice just kept on being beautiful."

"So that's the way it was," Miss Rachel whispered. She put out a timid hand toward the great Dane, but he ignored it. "Why is he waiting here, then?"

"The first Mrs. Terrice has moved in. On account of Brother Addison's will. It specified she must. Getting any ideas?"

"But—" Miss Rachel stopped to think. "No. Of course she couldn't have. She wasn't there when they did it."

"You've come round to my simple deduction, then, that the murder of Addison Brill was done by a trick. A trick with a bullet?"

She looked at him under the star-shine. "You said that you didn't want me to meddle with this case because I would end by confusing it. At the risk of making you angry again, I'm afraid that I shall have to say that I do not think it was simply a trick with a bullet. No murder can be just a trick with anything. There has to be motive, hatred, fear. There is a story behind even so simple a crime as stealing a loaf of bread, and there is an incredibly long story behind the murder of Mr. Brill."

Mayhew made a sound like a groan. "And all of the history of Mr. Brill must be unearthed before we can get down to facts and say to one of the Terrices, 'You killed Uncle Addison because he broke your piggy bank when you were four!'"

"You're making fun," she said softly.

"No. I didn't mean to. But Addison was killed, and one of the people present at the loading of that gun killed him. All that I need now—and I need him damned bad—is an eyewitness to the actual crime. I do not mean Mrs. Brenn. I want whoever it was that flapped and ran away. A man in a big coat, perhaps someone who had helped Addison get home. He usually seems to have begged rides from strangers."

"If I give you the person who looked at Addison and flapped," Miss Rachel said carefully, "will you let me stay on as the cook in that house?"

Mayhew took a long breath and seemed about to explode, and Miss Rachel hurried with the rest.

"Jennifer was the eyewitness to that murder. I tried to put you onto her before, you know. The glasses in the case that Pete pretended to find should have been Jennifer's; I meant them to be. Pete put a pair of Mr. Terrice's there instead. You might, also, have found a torn bit of Jennifer's taffeta skirt. She snagged it that night, perhaps on the Terrices' hedge."

"You knew all this," Mayhew ground out, "and didn't tell me?"

She lost a little of her patience. "You didn't let me tell you! You were just full of the idea that Addison had been killed with a trick bullet, as a sort of experiment or a bit of fun. You didn't want background or personalities or atmosphere. You wanted the crime explained as a magician would explain taking a rabbit out of a hat—not as one human being hating or revenging himself on another."

"Great—!" Mayhew, remembering the demure little old lady, choked on a string of expletives. "Why," he groaned, "does she have to happen to me?"

"Because you need me," Miss Rachel reminded. "Now listen and I'll tell you how to get hold of Jennifer. She's hiding, you see, to get away from me."

"That's one way of doing it," he muttered.

"But Jennifer's ideas of how to hide herself would be very simple indeed." Miss Rachel had turned on an inward look, as though mentally she were dissecting Miss Jennifer's mind. "She'd go to a hotel because she herself always gets lost in them—she thinks other people do too. She'd use an alias, one she liked and probably a name already in our family so that she wouldn't forget it."

"Like Miss Murd?" Mayhew wondered.

"Don't distract me. If I were you I'd start looking for Jennifer in some outlying large hotel, possibly one in Hollywood or in Santa Monica. For a start I'd work on the name of Standish. That was our mother's name, and Jennifer liked it."

He was a dark bulk that neither moved nor spoke. "Aren't you happy that I've figured things out for you?"

"You've been concealing a witness," he grumbled, "and burning evidence and Lord knows what else. Why don't you just go home and let me settle this?"

"When you start using your head," Miss Rachel said, "I might do that. When you start looking at something else besides that bullet."

"Why shouldn't I look at it? Here we have six people: Lydia and John Terrice, Thaw and Lee, your pet Miss Grant and an impertinent young pup named Pete. Addison is suspected to be on his way home, drunk as usual, and some one of the group gets the bright idea of scaring him by firing a pistol with a blank shell into his face as he opens the door. Who got the idea first? None of them seem to know. The one concrete bit of evidence in the whole mess is that bullet. I've had them re-enact the business of putting the shell in the gun four times, and each time they've done it differently, stood in different parts of the room, moved about and said new things. It's enough to drive a man crazy."

"They may not be doing it deliberately," she said thoughtfully. "I gather that the moment of putting the shell into the gun was one of pretty high emotional tension. Addison had been thoroughly obnoxious to all of them, so much so that the idea of scaring the wits out of him at the moment he came staggering in must have released all sorts of unholy joy. Even, I think, in Shirley, who is gentle to the point of being maddening."

"And yet you're asking me to find my way over a psychological tightrope to the murderer. When all of them, as you say, were cutting capers over the thought of sobering Addison up the hard way. When the one thing you can't avoid, the one thing you can depend on, was that the blank wasn't a blank, that the thing Mrs. Terrice popped into the pistol was a real bullet."

"You can't even depend on that, and that's the trouble with your theory. The gun, for instance, was Thaw's, and he must have brought it into the room. Suppose that it had a real bullet already concealed in the chamber, that he handed the gun to his mother in such a way that she couldn't see it. Did he, in any version of the gun loading, keep hold of the thing?"

"Twice," Mayhew growled, "he fixed it for her and sort of kept touching the barrel." He rubbed his head hard with the palm of one hand and stood up, making a dark shape between Miss Rachel and the lights of the kitchen. "Look, I'll go after Miss Jennifer. If I find her I can at least make sure that there was no one in the vestibule with Addison, no stranger we haven't tapped yet. That's the one possibility I want cleared up. The shenanigans with the pistol—I'll get them cleared up somehow."

Miss Rachel rose with him, a little figure inside the ghostly white of the cook's apron.

"There's one more thing you might try thinking about," she said.

"Yes?" Mayhew waited.

"Go and smell Miss Terrice's collection of perfumes," she suggested, "and let me know what ideas you have."

They began to walk across the dark lawn. "What's wrong with Miss Terrice's perfumes?"

"You mustn't look at it that way. While you're smelling, ask yourself what's wrong with Miss Terrice."

He groaned; a whine answered him from beneath the oleanders like an echo to grief.

"She may have no sense of smell whatever," Miss Rachel pointed out. "Or there may be some other explanation of what you'll find there."

A four-legged shape crept after them across the grass, as though waiting for further sounds from Mayhew. On the porch the big detective paused to look back into the yard. "Damned dog acts lonesome. Why don't they let him come in with his mistress?"

"I gathered that the present Mrs. Terrice doesn't care for dogs—or cats."

They watched while the dim yellow shape circled the lighted area and lay down finally in a patch of flowers. A broken whine drifted out upon the dark.

"Well, I've got to be off and get busy," Mayhew said, as if the dog's grief irked him. "Take care of yourself and stay out of trouble. I'll be here again in the morning. Good night."

He swung away by the side pathway, and for a long minute Miss Rachel stood still and watched the way he had gone. The yellow dog rose out of the patch of blossoms and sniffed at Mayhew's trail and then went back and crept into the greenery to whine. The moon had begun to lighten the sky. The Terrice house was quiet behind her, so quiet that she heard the ticking of a clock in the kitchen and the faint rustle of a vine on the porch as the wind blew it.

She went inside feeling a little chilled and lonely. She wondered whether she should risk peeping in upon the first Mrs. Terrice and then decided against it. There was still the question of getting into the cook's room, a problem that required time and ingenuity and in which she was, apparently, not going to have the co-operation of Lydia Terrice.

The second floor was utterly quiet and empty, and in the third floor she found darkness. She groped her way to Shirley's door, wondering meanwhile why the light should have been turned off and not liking it, and then some other impression stopped her, a breath out of the dark, a movement of air that was unfamiliar until she recalled the draft that had touched her ankles from under the cook's door.

She turned about and saw, like two eyes in the gloom, the pale light of windows. There was, too, the spindling outline of a bedstead, the bulk of other furniture beginning to show under the moonrise.

"It's open!" she heard herself whisper, and felt the little irregularity of the doorsill under her foot and smelled the stuffy odor of a closed room. She was inside. She was inside where she had wanted to be, and now all that she had to do was to look about.

She pushed the door shut silently behind her and stood waiting while the room brightened with the eerie light, while a patch of moonglow came to rest beside the bed like a little rug, and while the huge old-fashioned dresser, the closet door, the shabby table and old chair emerged from darkness.

She had opened the top drawer of the dresser and had found it as stuffed as Shirley's own and was sorting the contents little by little when she heard a movement from the hall. With her hands full of papers and scraps of clothing and some odds and ends of old fishing tackle she went to the door and put her ear to it.

The moon made a long rectangle that reached almost to her feet, and the night was so utterly still that she thought at first she might, incredibly, still be hearing the tick of the clock in the kitchen.

Then she knew the tick and the pause for what they were, and fear crawled over her like the stroke of an icy hand along her flesh.

There was nothing reasonable about that fear—nothing sane. It was the sort of terror that takes refuge in the wearing of garlic, in the reciting of incantations by candlelight.

For the clicking sound in the hall was an animal sound. It was the noise that a dog—*or something else*—would make with his toenails on the bare borders of the hall.

14

SHIRLEY STIRRED upon the bed and rose up and made a slim silhouette against the window.

"It must be fearfully late," she murmured. "I feel as if I'd slept for hours. Where have you been?"

Miss Rachel, slipping out of her petticoats, decided not to tell Shirley about the silly cowardice that had kept her crouched in the cook's room with her ear to the door panel. It *had* been cowardice, and it *was* silly, she thought annoyedly. A woman of seventy—really practically seventy-one—had no business hearing things like werewolves in the hall and sitting in the moonlight for hours with her eyes glued on the door as though the werewolf might jump in at her. And it had been madness, too, to think that sly steps had come up from the lower hall and had led the werewolf thing away.

She folded the third petticoat over a chair and sat down to remove her shoes, but her mind skirted back through the recent hours to the discoveries she had made across the hall.

The first thing she had found of any importance was a bottle such as druggists provide with prescriptions, having a medicine dropper built into the cap. The bottle, uncorked, had smelled faintly of a turpentinelike mixture. Miss Rachel had wrapped it carefully in a bit of cloth and stowed it in the pocket of the cook's apron.

The second discovery had been the small box with the scarlet stripe lying empty on the floor under the window, beside it a ball of cotton like a little nest.

The third, the one she liked least because it had held her gaze throughout the vigil by the door, had been a wreath of garlic pinned securely to the wall over the cook's bed. Dry and dusty, filmed with a breath of cobweb, it had cast a black halo on the moonlit space and had brought into the room all of the middle-Europe frightfulness at which Miss Rachel had previously scoffed.

She slipped into bed and tucked the little box and the bottle wrapped in cloth beneath her pillow. The garlic she had left firmly behind. Werewolves, she thought, couldn't come into Parchly Heights. Parchly Heights simply wouldn't let them.

But in the dreams she had during the remainder of the night strange phantoms drifted, and the memory of the toe-nailed thing in the hall returned more vivid than when she had been awake, and the sly steps on the stairs were recognizable, and a face she knew looked in at the door of the cook's room and grinned at her.

She awoke suddenly to find it was morning and that Shirley stood at the dresser pulling a comb through her thick hair.

"Mmmmm. . . ." Shirley said through a mouthful of bobby pins. "Pete's starting breakfast for us. You look tired. Where did you disappear to during dinner?"

"I was—just scouting," Miss Rachel answered.

"Pete asked me if I thought you'd be leaving."

"He did, did he?" Miss Rachel sat up and looked interested. "And why did he think I might?"

"He said no lady could stand it. Stand cooking for the Terrices, I guess. He likes you, you know. He's afraid you'll have your feelings hurt."

"Complete indifference doesn't hurt. Unless, of course," Miss Rachel added, thinking of Shirley, "you're lonely."

"I've been lonely," Shirley said, looking at her own reflection in the mirror. "If it hadn't been for Pete—and Thaw too. He has queer spells of seeming to want to make up for all his rudeness. But for Uncle John or Aunt Lydia or Lee—I might just as well never have lived."

"With Lee it may be a case of jealousy," Miss Rachel said.

"Jealous? Of me?"

"I think so. An obscure kind of jealousy, a little hard to define."

"But she's beautiful; she has everything."

"She doesn't seem to have many friends."

"Well—no." Shirley frowned. "Sometimes she gives parties, and a lot of young people come. But no one ever comes alone, I mean as a friend would. A girl. Or just one fellow." She pulled the comb through a ruffle of dark hair. "Just now she's between boy friends. She is every once in a while."

"Psychologically she is amazingly like Mrs. Terrice."

Shirley nodded; a whistle drifted upstairs, and she began to finish her hair hurriedly. "There's Pete. He needs us."

Miss Rachel let Shirley hurry away while she finished dressing. She needed a safe place for the bottle which had held paint thinner and the little box with its cotton wadding in which was a faint round impress like the shape of a ring. She ended by going to the closet and peeping in; the big pockets of the red robe shone whitely at the end of the shadowy space, and Miss Rachel ran a tentative hand into one of them.

Her fingers encountered a small hard cylinder that turned under their touch with a cool metallic smoothness. She drew the thing forth. It was a large-caliber bullet.

Miss Rachel went back and sat down suddenly on the edge of the bed and looked at the things in her palm. There was the little box with its cotton wadding (an odd place for a ring) and the bottle with its smell of paint thinner, and a bullet. The box and the paint thinner had been in an unoccupied room, but the bullet had been in Shirley's newest and most prized possession. Had Shirley just not had time to get rid of the thing?

The idea shook Miss Rachel so that she shivered, and she looked about at the room, at the space where Miss Muffet had hung with the face of a werewolf meant to shine by night, and at the shabby plainness of the bed and of the other furnishings.

A most peculiar light came into her eyes, and she rose briskly and went back to the closet, and into the pockets of the red robe she put all three of her little clues. When she had finished dressing she went briskly downstairs with her cat following.

In the kitchen Mr. Terrice was by the stove and Shirley was facing him. There was subtle antagonism in the look he gave Miss Rachel. His spare voice finished what he had to say to Shirley: "If you feel so strongly about it, let it go. You act, Shirley, as though I were trying to rob you."

"It isn't that at all," Shirley stumbled, looking miserable. "I—I just want time to think about the stock and what I should do with it."

"As you say." He shot another glance at Miss Rachel, as though trying to discover some source of Shirley's refusal.

"Ah—Miss Murd. I'm afraid I'll have to ask a favor of you this morning. We have a guest in the house. I—I haven't explained her presence to Mrs. Terrice as yet and I thought—just for breakfast, perhaps—you wouldn't mind slipping upstairs with a tray for her."

Miss Rachel, tying an apron that all but engulfed her, looked simple. "A lady, Mr. Terrice? Would she be a relative?"

"Ah—yes. A relative." ("The man is smirking," Miss Rachel thought, "at his own little joke.") "She won't require much. A bit of melon and some coffee. Last room to your right, at the front. Understand, I'll have things straightened out by lunch time."

"It's quite all right, sir." Miss Rachel took a tray from a cupboard. "I'll attend to it at once."

He thanked her dryly and went away, and Shirley watched while Miss Rachel flew at the task of getting the tray arranged.

"What could he have meant?" she wondered. "Who could it be upstairs?"

"The first Mrs. Terrice," Miss Rachel whispered. "Come home again. Where she belonged, I think. No wonder I said the family seemed as though it didn't belong together. Thaw, I noticed, was careful never to call Lydia his mother."

"He doesn't, does he?" Shirley poured coffee into a cup. "How did you happen to know, though, before Mr. Terrice told you?"

"I have ways," Miss Rachel said mysteriously, and watched Shirley's eyes widen. "I know a great deal that I don't go about shouting over. Hidden things. In the queerest places."

The gaze that met her own had no faltering and no guilt in it. With a little sigh Miss Rachel put a snowy napkin over the contents of the tray and went off upstairs. The last door to the right . . . She noticed, tapping, that the cat had followed her.

There was no answer to her knock. She gave the knob a turn,

and the door swung in and she saw the drawn shades, the big bed with its silky spread, the disorder of dropped clothing on the floor.

"Mrs. Terrice?" she whispered, having some idea of the woman skulking in the shadows as she had done upon the lawn, sallow face averted, red hands twisted against her skirt. "I have breakfast for you. Are you here?"

The cat frightened her, howling suddenly on a dolorous note out of utter stillness, and Miss Rachel put the tray on the dressing table and went to the door to the bathroom. She rapped again. "Mrs. Terrice?"

The room kept its hollow silence. She put the tips of her fingers against the door to the bath and saw a slowly widening triangle of blue tile, the fluffy edges of a mat. A breath of air stirred up from behind the door held a strange sickening odor.

Miss Rachel felt her own hand shake as she pushed the door again. The bit of blue tile became a square that showed the corner of the tub, the pulled edge of the shower curtain hanging and torn, and something else—a print. A paw print. A long paw print made in blood.

The blue tile swung in fuzzy circles, and the edge of the torn shower curtain hung on its perimeter like a pattern in a kaleidoscope. Miss Rachel was conscious of terror and illness and a desire not to see what else it was that lay inside the bathroom. She went and sat on the stool of the dressing table and took a long sip of the hot coffee she had brought up on the tray. The cat had gone back to the hall and stood there, waiting, with every hair along her spine on edge.

"I should have known," she thought miserably. "I should have guessed. Addison may have known who meant to kill him. He would have told her."

She forced herself to get off the white leather stool and go to the bathroom door and push it wide.

Lissa Terrice lay half crouched on her face in the center of the floor. She was wrapped—what was left of her—in an imitation-silk kimono whose pale color had soaked up rivers of blood. The dull hair was flung up and off her neck, and her hands covered her ears and chin. There was a dumb air of pleading, of submission, in the way her body had fallen.

And about her, a design in scarlet, were the long paw prints of the thing that had walked in blood.

Miss Rachel went in carefully to touch the slashed flesh, to make sure that no life stayed there. The skin of Lissa Terrice's shoulder was startlingly cold. Miss Rachel, remembering the bed with its silky cover still in place and the drawn shades, knew suddenly that Mrs. Terrice had been dead throughout the night—that perhaps at the very moment she had gone upstairs to find the cook's room open Death and his weapon had been at work here.

She went out and shut the door on the crouched bloody thing with its strange border of paw prints and found an extension telephone on a small table in the hall. Mayhew answered at last, brisk and businesslike, and then listened in dead silence while she told him what she had found.

"Stay there. Stay in the room with it. I'll be out in ten minutes." There was a sound as though he had flung the receiver at the hook.

Miss Rachel pushed the phone away, but she did not do as Mayhew had told her. She ran upstairs into the third floor and tried the door of the cook's room and found it locked. Kneeling, she recalled suddenly that once the lock had had a plug of cotton in it—cotton like that in the little box where the faint outline of something like a ring remained.

She went scurrying back downstairs and through the door to the bathroom and endured again the sight of Lissa Terrice in her bloody death. With a gentle movement she drew out the clenched left hand. The nails had dribbled scarlet on the tile beneath. Not blood. . . . She saw the smear of polish on the other palm. On one finger was the ring, a wink of yellow in the light.

For a moment the odor, the flesh in rumpled rayon, the thumping pulse in her own heart almost caused her to faint. Then, forcing herself, she drew off the ring and studied the initials inside it. *J. A. T. to L. B.*

Back in Shirley's room she took the little box from the pocket of the robe, removed the lid with its red stripe, fitted the ring into its nest upon the cotton.

Then she sat quietly and waited. There was no sound below to tell of the discovery of Lissa Terrice's body until the police car wailed to a halt outside. Then there was a burst of steps and Shirley came in. She was enormous-eyed and pale; she fell on the bed and put her head into Miss Rachel's lap.

"You saw her?" Miss Rachel asked.

Shirley trembled. "I went looking for you. It's the first Mrs. Terrice, isn't it? Did you"—she made a strangled sound—"did you see the marks on the floor?"

"Be quiet," Miss Rachel said, stroking her hair. "Listen."

There was movement now on the second floor; they listened for long minutes while the police tramped back and forth and more sirens arrived in the street.

Mayhew came up at last to fill the door like a brown bear

with a chip on his shoulder. He took them in with a glance. "Not so frisky? I thought you wouldn't be. Mrs. Terrice isn't pretty, but you would have her. Tell me what you know."

Shirley said brokenly, "I didn't even see her until she was dead."

Miss Rachel pushed her up. "Go to the bathroom and bathe your eyes and take an aspirin." When Shirley had gone out she said to Mayhew: "Mr. Terrice sent me up with a breakfast tray. I looked for her—and there she was."

Mayhew lifted the little box. "What have we here?"

"Her ring. I took it off."

He stopped in the act of sitting down by her, and his big hand holding the box had a sudden look of anger to it.

"No, don't scold yet," she went on. "I had found the box in the cook's room across the hall. There was a print in the cotton wadding made by a ring. Shirley thinks she has seen the box before; she doesn't recall where. I think it's been kept hidden in the cook's room to have it ready for a purpose. Tell me, was Mrs. Terrice—Lissa Terrice—wearing a ring last night when you saw her?"

Mayhew frowned. "No, I'm sure that she wasn't. She was putting on nail polish, and I think I would have seen a ring if she'd had one. But what of it?"

"The ring was bait, I think," Miss Rachel said. The sound of hysterics had begun to float up from the second-floor hall—Mrs. Terrice's soprano, quite out of control, and Mr. Terrice's agitated murmurs on a lower note. "You see, the situation was made for it. Lissa Terrice had come home to more than one kind of heritage. To Addison's money, in the first place. To Thaw's loyalty, certainly; to Lee's, perhaps. To a position in the family that was rightfully hers—represented by a wedding ring. Someone came to offer her the final gift last night; must obviously have come in the guise of a friend. You might try finding who had kept the ring for her all of these years."

Mayhew put the ring into his pocket with a kind of impatience. "Then they must have gotten to her damned fast. She was kicking off her shoes when I left her. Someone struck her down before she was ever in the tub."

"And before her nails had dried," Miss Rachel said, remembering the red smears.

Mayhew had stood up abruptly. "Thanks for your ideas about the ring. I'll try to find who had it. I'll get your statement into the record later. Just now I'm anxious to get hold of the Terrice family and hear their stories. Someone took a big chance ducking into that room almost the moment I'd left it. I'm going to try to find out who that someone was."

"He's still looking for that hat with the rabbit in it," Miss Rachel thought, listening to his heavy steps on the stairs. "I almost wish he'd find it. Two heads and all."

15

Miss Rachel returned the box to the pocket of the red robe, waited until Mayhew should have had time to settle himself somewhere below, and then went down cautiously to the second floor. There were two uniformed policemen in the hall, and the sound of Mrs. Terrice's hysterics was quite distinct. Mr. Terrice stood by the table with the telephone, staring at the instrument as though trying to think of someone to call—a doctor for Mrs. Terrice, possibly. The fringe of hair over one ear was ruffled, and his tie was awry; strange disarray, indeed, for the sleekness of Mr. Terrice.

Miss Rachel slipped down the back stairs and stood still in the pantry to listen. Lieutenant Mayhew's bass voice reached her from the other side of the door to the dining room. He was explaining some point of evidence in the peculiarly patient and forgiving tone that meant he yearned and was about ready to pounce upon an unsuspecting victim.

She put an eye to the crack and found herself looking at the lieutenant and at Lee Terrice. The girl sitting opposite was wearing a blue angora sweater and gray slacks; her pale hair was pushed into a pompadour from which curls escaped. She looked composed and a little disgusted.

"I agree with what you say," she told Mayhew, "but I'm not psychic. It's true I might have been suspicious about seeing you come out of Addison's room. I was. I even admit glancing inside after you had disappeared. I'd just come up from dinner when I saw you leave."

"But you didn't see anything?" Mayhew prompted.

"I didn't see anything," she agreed. "I've told you that I didn't. The light was on. I presumed you'd forgotten to turn it off and I did so. I remember thinking that the room looked disorderly and that Shirley should be asked to straighten it. That's all. As I said, I'm not psychic. I couldn't know instinctively that there was a dead woman in the bathroom."

Mayhew seemed to study the smooth expressionless features, the carefully rouged mouth, and the steady eyes.

"And you deny knowing that your mother was here until the time of the discovery of her body?"

She made a slight impatient gesture with one hand. "I— There is something I may as well explain to you now, Lieutenant. I don't—I've never felt about Lissa as though she were my mother. Perhaps that seems ghastly to you now, seeing that the poor woman is dead. It's just that I'm trying to be honest about the situation. I didn't love Lissa. She left me when I was a baby, turned me over to Lydia, who has loved and cared for me all of my life."

"Perhaps you had never had things fully explained to you," Mayhew said. "Perhaps your father and your step-mother weren't quite fair."

She shook her head. "I'm sure that they were, Mr. Mayhew. I haven't been unduly influenced by Thaw's histrionics. He's always been a rebel and a nuisance. I've never let him sway me about Lydia. She's been wonderful. And that—that other woman just didn't keep herself presentable. Not ever."

"How long had it been," Mayhew said, very much under control, "since you had seen your—this other creature?"

Scarlet flew into her face at that; one hand made a convulsive move before it slid into her slacks pocket. "Not long," she got out. "Not over a week or so. That was the day I asked Thaw not to bring her inside again."

"He was in the habit of bringing her inside this house?"

"Yes. I felt it wasn't the thing to do, and I asked him to stop it. I had some sorority friends to tea that day. There could have been embarrassing consequences."

Mayhew fiddled with the notebook on his knee. He looked, Miss Rachel thought, ridiculously like a bear trying to read a primer. But his stare was innocent, almost blank. "You might like to know, Miss Terrice, that this—ah—dead woman made a will. Odd, wasn't it, that she should die thinking of you?" He had fished out a dirty piece of paper. "Of course it isn't written on very good stationery. People like that wouldn't know the difference, I guess. She just scribbled a few lines to the effect that in case anything happened to her you were to have all of her share in Addison's estate."

Chalk-white and still as stone, she looked at him. The light from the windows, through which blew the faint breath of stock, picked out the tightening of her throat, the pressure of teeth on the inner surfaces of her lips. "I—I don't believe—"

"I'll read it to you," Mayhew said carelessly. "It isn't long. It may not, in fact, be even legal so far as being drawn properly. But it expresses a certain sentiment I feel you should know." He read slowly: "*I hereby leave and bequeath all of my interest in my*

*brother Addison's estate to my little girl, Lee Terrice, for her use alone.
Signed, Lissa Brill Terrice."*

"I—I didn't know. She didn't act—"

He cut in as though he had not heard her stumbling words. "Mothers are peculiar creatures. Like dogs. They never seem to know when they're not wanted."

She turned so that he should not see her face. "Is that all?"

"No," Mayhew said suddenly. "I want to know why you won't admit seeing your mother last night before she died."

"I didn't see her," she flamed.

"You were heard talking to her."

She started to jerk out an answer and then fell still. She looked at Mayhew slowly, measuring him. "What did you say?"

"You were heard talking to your mother in Addison's room after I had gone."

"By whom?" She waited, and Mayhew pretended delay in finding a certain page in his notebook. "Wait. I know who it was. It was Shirley. She was on the stairs to the third floor when I came out." Lee's voice was shaking, furious. "She'd be the one who tried to get me into trouble. She's just a tramp; she hasn't any home, any background. She's tried over and over to make herself liked, to wheedle sympathy out of us. Those ridiculous accidents—"

"Yes?" Mayhew prompted.

"She did them herself, of course. Now she's lying about me out of jealousy. I won't take it."

"You don't have to," Mayhew said smoothly. "Miss Grant had nothing to say about your whereabouts. I haven't as yet spoken to her."

"You—" Miss Rachel could see Lee's mind going back furiously through what she had just said; there was a bitter look of being trapped to her. "You led me on. You've lied to me."

Mayhew was imperturbably putting the scrap of paper back into the notebook. He looked vaguely like a father bear counting his money. "No, Miss Terrice, I haven't lied to you. But you've lied to me. Why won't you tell me about the interview with your mother?"

She stood up, quivering, and her hands caught at the neck of the fragile sweater and pulled it into a wad. "I wasn't with my mother! I didn't see her!"

"You saw her clothes scattered about the bedroom. You must have. If you went in when you said you did, directly I'd disappeared, you must have found her still undressing."

"You went upstairs," Lee panted. "I went to the foot of the back stairs and listened to find out what you were doing. You went into a room up there—I don't know which one—and you stayed a moment and then came down. I hurried back along the hall so that you wouldn't know I'd been sp—been watching you. I ducked into *that* room and waited until you went on down in the direction of the kitchen."

"You were in there, then, for a minute or two?"

"Y-yes." Her eyes slid away from his. "Yes, I suppose I was."

"Yet you heard no movement, no sound from the bathroom, no water running? Nothing at all?"

"Nothing at all," she stammered.

He slapped the book shut. "Thank you, Miss Terrice. I'll talk to you again later."

She hooked her thumbs through her slacks belt in a belated effort at insouciance. "You'll tell me first who's lying about me, who's saying they heard a quarrel between me and—and Lissa?"

"A quarrel?" He looked innocence at her. "No quarrel, Miss Terrice. You're mistaken there."

"Then who—?"

"And I'll have to protect, for the time being, the identity of the person who spoke to me about the matter."

"He's lying, of course," Miss Rachel told herself, knowing Mayhew of old. She left the crack in the door before Lee could reach it, and scurried through the pantry and into the kitchen, bright with sun, where Pete sat on the edge of the sink staring gloomily at his toes.

"Messy affair, isn't it?" he greeted her. "I wish Shirley hadn't gone barging up to look for you. She shouldn't see things like that."

"Have you seen the dead woman?" Miss Rachel asked.

He nodded. "Before. *And* after." He slid off the sink to stand facing her. "Uncle John brought her in last night through this back door. Aunt Lydia had me polishing silver in the dining room, and I saw them go past the pantry door on the way to the back stairs. She had on the most awful red hat, but there was something new in her face. I'd seen her before, you know, off and on, though I knew I wasn't supposed to have. Well, last night she had a hopeful expression. A kind of rejuvenation. I can't explain it any better than that. It made me think, somehow, that getting into the house had meant a lot to her."

"I guess it did," Miss Rachel said thoughtfully. "By the way, what of the dog? Was he with her?"

"Not inside," Pete said. "Aunt Lydia hates animals. I heard him whining out in the dark last night. I guess he's still hanging about somewhere."

Miss Rachel went out upon the back porch and surveyed the

sunny yard, where wide lawns led away to flower beds and the vegetable patches behind the garage. Two butterflies hovered above a bed of petunias, huge double blooms of smoky rose, and a bee made a darting fleck of gold. There was no groveling yellow shape as there had been last night. She picked a pathway through to the rear of the gardens and stood and whistled softly. But no mournful eyes looked through shrubbery at her, and no whine answered.

At last, under a hydrangea, she found a hollowed spot where something had lain. On a single fallen leaf was a smear of red, dried dark stuff with a faint crack through it. Miss Rachel crushed the leaf to dust and went back upstairs.

She peeped in at Lee Terrice's doorway and found the big room in order, the bed made and the blinds drawn up to let in the light. The mirrored panels which concealed the closet were drawn back, and Miss Rachel spent some time among the clothes that hung inside. Sniffing, mostly.

When she had finished her examination of Lee Terrice's wardrobe she went and sat down before the dressing tables and studied the multicolored perfume bottles. A flagon of clear yellow, with a top shaped like a brown pansy and a label that said "Sunny Day" attracted her interest at last, and she seemed to regard it with a dreamy abstraction—abstraction that endured so long that she was still sitting there when the door opened.

She jumped up, scarlet, but it was Mayhew who looked in at her. "Hiding?" he wondered. "Miss Terrice wouldn't like your being here, I think."

She beckoned him. "Come in. You haven't smelled Miss Terrice's perfumes as I told you to. I know you haven't or you would have asked her about them downstairs."

He picked up a near one, unscrewed it, and smelled the contents. "Must be getting a cold," he said. "I can't smell a damned thing." He put it down to try another. "Is it me or is it them?"

"It's them," Miss Rachel said. "Don't touch that yellow one. It just might possibly have fingerprints, though I doubt it. Most of them are simply tinted water. It isn't. It's nail-polish remover, and a lot of it is gone since I was here last."

Mayhew stared at her. "What's the idea? Is Miss Terrice nuts?"

Miss Rachel shook her head sweetly. "No. She's proud. Her own version of what to be proud of—stuffy things that mean money. She used to have it—they all used to have it. Now they don't. Not until Addison's estate gets settled."

Mayhew fumbled through the rest of the bottles, made faces at several. "You mean she ran out of perfume and so just stuck in anything that came handy? This one smells like dry cleaner."

"A few of the bottles contain useful things—nail-polish remover, something to fix spots in clothing, a lotion, an astringent. Miss Terrice wouldn't like us to know about this. She'd want us to think that all of the perfume was real."

He took a handkerchief and picked up the yellow bottle with care by its brown pansy cap and studied the tablespoon or so of contents in its bottom. "A remover for nail polish, eh?" He frowned. "Any ideas?"

"You said that Lissa Terrice was putting polish on her nails while you talked with her last night. I noticed, in removing the ring, that the wet polish had been smeared before it had dried. It occurred to me that some of that polish might have stuck to the murderer—to his or her clothes. That a lot of polish remover might have been needed. So I thought of Miss Terrice and her bottles."

"And you recall how full this was?"

"None were as low as that when I was here before. It seems to me that the bottle with the pansy cap was almost full."

"We'll check on this then." He took the bottle and went away to where other men could doubtless immediately test it for fingerprints.

Miss Rachel, without any conscience that she was aware of, began rummaging quickly in Miss Terrice's dresser drawers.

Under the tissue paper in the bottom of the third she found a sheet of paper which had been rumpled and then straightened out. Its writing matched other writing of Lee's in a date book. It began:

PETE:

I intend to tell the police about your quarrel with Addison. I heard most of it, you see, and I feel sure that it had something to do with Addison's being killed the very next evening.

I remember most distinctly that Addison said to you, "I think you'd better cut it out. You'll be getting into real trouble. What would Thaw say?"

And you cursed him.

Now if you can offer any explanation . . .

The note ended without conclusion, as though Miss Terrice might have regretted any willingness to listen to Pete's side of the quarrel. It had been rumpled, then smoothed and put away here for safekeeping. Had Lee decided to keep it on hand, to debate on offering her information to the police?

Miss Rachel slid the drawer shut and tucked the note into the pocket of her apron. She was, she decided, going to have to do something about her collection of clues. She had a bullet, a box which had contained an old wedding ring, a bottle which had held paint thinner, a blood-stained leaf, and now a letter.

She was almost at the door when there was a rap on it, a soft but imperative knock that had, somehow, a hint of secrecy in it.

Miss Rachel cast about and wondered if she could make it to the bathroom or into the closet behind Lee Terrice's clothes. The room, so richly furnished, was astonishingly bare of hiding places. The rattle of the doorknob sent her flying across the room to the other side of the bed. She lay down just as the door opened. With a rustle of petticoats that seemed as loud as cannon fire, she slid beneath the quilted coverlet into the darkness and dust of under the bed.

Whatever Shirley was, she was not a thorough housekeeper.

Miss Rachel held her nose to keep from sneezing.

Footsteps sounded on the carpet of Lee Terrice's room—oddly quiet steps that caused Miss Rachel to lie suddenly still, to feel suddenly rather afraid.

There was the tinkle and click of glass touching other glass.

Someone was at Lee Terrice's dressing table among the bottles that were supposed to hold perfume.

16

THE DOOR opened and Mayhew's voice boomed: "Where is she? Oh. Terrice, since you're here, I'd like to ask a few questions."

Mr. Terrice's voice, as smooth as silk, replied: "Why, certainly, officer. Were you, though, looking for my daughter?"

"Ah—yes." Miss Rachel could imagine Mayhew's stare about the room, his mental query as to her whereabouts. There wasn't any dignified way to let him know; she would not have Mr. Terrice's spectacles peering at her under the bed. "Yes. Your daughter. She can wait until another time, however. Just now I want the details of your first wife's entry into this house. Last night, I believe, wasn't it?"

Mr. Terrice coughed slightly. "Shall we sit down? We may as well talk in comfort." The bedsprings creaked under Mayhew's enormous settling, and Miss Rachel looked at them with worry. Mr. Terrice seemed to have taken the hassock by the radio, from the glimpse she had of his shining shoes. "About my first wife, Lissa. There was to be some delay in the settlement of Addison's estate, you see. He's being buried today—I guess you know that. It was planned to read his will and to start the estimates of his property immediately afterward. A most awkward procedure, I think. The estate was to be evaluated as to its total, certain percentages figured out, Lissa to have first choice of about half of it—whatever properties she wished to make her share. This, naturally, involved considerable delay."

"Whose idea was it that she should wait here in your home?"

"Ah—mine. The terms of Addison's will were that Lissa should be kept advised of all moves in the settlement. The easiest way to do this was simply to have her here. Otherwise, there were certain clauses which might have been interpreted to—to remove other claims entirely."

Miss Rachel thought of Mr. Terrice, neat as a pin, meticulous, leading in his ex-wife in her dreadful hat. His mind had been on Addison's money, of course; the money that might escape him if he weren't careful.

"How many members of the family knew of Lissa Terrice's presence here?" Mayhew asked.

"Only myself. I told no one. I had intended telling them today, after breakfast, at some propitious moment. Lydia, I felt, might—well, the situation might be awkward. You know, I presume, that I divorced one sister to marry the other. There were—well, feelings under the surface that might not best come into the open."

How hard it must be, Miss Rachel considered, for the Mr. Terrices of the world—quiet bloodless people with a flair for order—to keep their lives quite as emotionless as they would like. The woman in the red hat—there would have been times when she must have protested being put away, when aloneness and poverty and shabby living had made her hard to control.

"What are your theories about her death?" Mayhew asked, as though certain Mr. Terrice had some.

"Theories? I'm afraid—" He hesitated. "I can't even quite believe that Lissa is dead, much less have theories about how she died. You said that she had had her throat cut. I presume you're sure it wasn't suicide."

"It wasn't suicide," Mayhew told him. "Someone stood behind her and reached to the front and drew the knife from left to right and almost cut her head off. Then they did a little extra work beyond that, to make sure that she was dead, or else in spite."

Mr. Terrice's feet moved nervously on the carpet.

"She was killed in the bath of the room formerly occupied by Addison Brill. The knife seems to have been laid for a while on the edge of the tub. The blade, I judge, was about seven inches long. Your nephew Pete says that there was such a knife in the kitchen and that it has now disappeared."

"Pete—you can't depend on him."

"Nevertheless, I am inclined to believe that Mrs. Terrice was killed with a weapon near at hand. Her arrival here was not, as you say, expected by the other members of your family. Therefore, the murder must have been an impromptu affair, as it were."

Mr. Terrace choked. "Ridiculous! You cannot accuse one of us of having killed her. What motive had we?"

"Money, for one," Mayhew said briskly. "Lissa Terrice's share of Addison's wealth goes to her daughter. Your daughter, too, by the way."

"To Lee?" The note of incredulity in Mr. Terrice's voice struck Miss Rachel with the impact of a bullet. "But—how odd. How very odd." He took time to think over its oddness. "Was it—? Would you mind telling me whether it was a recent will?"

"It was not a recent will," Mayhew said, and Miss Rachel realized that he had been lying, in more than one respect, to Lee. He'd wanted her to think her mother had died almost before the ink was dry. But this statement of his would account for the dirty paper, the tattered look of the sheet he had tucked into his notebook.

"Had you thought," Mr. Terrice went on after a while for consideration, "that Mrs. Terrice's death might not have been due to a desire for her share of the estate at all? She might, for instance, have known something about Addison's murder and been killed for that—to keep her silent."

"I had thought of that angle," Mayhew admitted guardedly.

"You see," Mr. Terrice went on, warming a little, "there were some unpleasant factors in Addison's getting killed. Not that I'd offer a young girl as a—ah—victim, or anything like that. But Shirley had had trouble with him, and she's an emotional child and may have been overwhelmed with emotion and just—er—done something unfortunate."

"Hmmmmm," Mayhew said. "She's emotional, you say?"

"Very. And in case you've forgotten, it was she who went upstairs and brought down the bullets for Thaw's pistol. The bullet that killed Addison must have been among the others."

"Which were all blanks when we examined them," Mayhew said thoughtfully.

"But not *that* bullet. It was a real shell, and it killed my brother-in-law, and Shirley brought it for Mrs. Terrice to put into the gun."

"Unfortunate, wasn't it, that Mrs. Terrice should have picked out of the box just the bullet Shirley meant her to."

Mr. Terrice made haste to cover his error. "A point you never settled entirely, Lieutenant. If you recall, there was some question as to whether Shirley had not actually handed Mrs. Terrice *one* bullet."

"I do recall it," Mayhew said with warmth; the bed squeaked as though he had moved suddenly in anger. "But, to get to the point, you're suggesting now that Shirley murdered Mrs. Lissa Terrice because the woman knew she had murdered Addison."

"Nothing of the sort," Mr. Terrice said. "I was trying to point out that there are other possibilities than the one you're so bent on following. You simply refuse to see Shirley or Pete in the circle of suspects. I can't understand why."

"I keep thinking about all that money," Mayhew answered. "Don't you?"

A stunned silence on Mr. Terrice's part lasted more than a minute. "I—I don't feel in any mood for humor, Lieutenant. If you please."

"I'm not trying to be funny." Mayhew's boom was filled with impatience. "Two people have been killed here, and I want to know why. You suggest that one was killed because he made amorous advances to a young girl while he was drunk and that the other was killed because she knew the girl did it. Well, it could be true. I handled a case last month in which a man was killed because he had a two-hundred-dollar life-insurance policy."

"You mean the motive I've offered is too trivial?" Mr. Terrice said stiffly.

"It is flimsy," Mayhew said.

"I'm afraid that you're underestimating the emotions of the very young. Shirley, you see— Well, we've rather suspected that the child was on the verge of being neurotic. There were a few things happened—accidents, we thought them—that might have been caused by Shirley's desire for sympathy. She's an or-phan, alone, and she may have been psychologically unbalanced for a while. Addison could certainly be obnoxious. I—perhaps I shouldn't mention this without asking Pete about it first—but Pete and Addison had an awful row over Shirley the day before Addison died."

"You should have told me this before," Mayhew growled.

"Well, it might not have meant anything. I merely bring it up now to show that the feeling of the young people over the way Addison had acted was pretty strong. Pete was just—well, livid."

"And the quarrel was about Shirley?"

"In some way." A trace of puzzlement reflected itself in Mr. Terrice's tone. "I didn't hear the whole argument. Addison was threatening to tell something."

"To Shirley?"

"No." Caution came, and Miss Rachel remembered the note in Lee's dresser and its words: *What would Thaw say?* Mr. Ter-rice went on: "As I say, I didn't get all of it."

"And you're bringing it in now to show that there was strong feeling against Addison. Do you mean on Pete's part?"

"Ah—Pete and Shirley. Though Pete wasn't afraid of him and Shirley was, you see, and that might make a difference in their behavior." A pause while Mr. Terrice seemed to grope for words—neat, precise words with which to dissect other people. "My brother-in-law had let drink get the better of him. He had deteriorated. Things were rapidly reaching the point where we couldn't have stood him much longer."

"And so he was murdered," Mayhew said thoughtfully.

"I mean we should have asked him to live elsewhere," Mr. Terrice added quickly. "Murder wasn't the—the thing we had in mind."

"Someone had it in mind."

"Well, she's an emotional child. One mustn't blame her too much."

Mayhew made a sound like a bear with a sore foot who has the foot stepped on. "I won't keep you any longer," he said. "You might go and find out if Mrs. Terrice is in condition to talk to me now."

Mr. Terrice, after some delay, made a reluctant departure. Mayhew began to walk about the room; Miss Rachel heard his steps on the tile of the bathroom, and she took the moment when his back was turned to slide out from under the bed. When Mayhew came back and found her standing there he looked at her as though she had risen out of the floor.

"Where in the devil were you? Behind the wallpaper?"

"I made myself invisible," Miss Rachel snapped, because she was a little cross at his slowness. "Why aren't you working on Pete with everything you've got?"

"You mean because of the argument he had with Addison? Yes, I'm getting around to that immediately."

Miss Rachel took the note in Lee's handwriting out of her apron pocket. "If Pete doesn't crack you might go on to Lee and Thaw. One of them ought to know what the argument was about."

He read the note while she told him where she had found it. "What about Pete?" he asked. "What's he doing here? Why isn't he working? God knows jobs are plentiful."

"Pete's independence is all on the surface. He's actually a leaner. He's leaned on the Terrices so long he can't imagine getting out and shifting for himself. He's been telling Shirley lately that if she had a bit of money they could go away together."

"And has Shirley got the bit of money?"

"She might. I'm waiting for a letter from my bankers—I may find it at home if I can slip off there. Speaking of home, what of Jennifer? Did you find her?"

"Just before I came out here there was a report that a Mrs. Standish was staying at the Florentine in Beverly Hills. She moved in yesterday wearing a heavy veil and hasn't stuck her head out of her room since. The chambermaid thinks she's living on crackers. Something tells me it's Miss Jennifer."

"It's undoubtedly Jennifer, though I didn't dream she'd be as bad as that. What are you going to do about her?"

"With your permission, I'd like to scare the wits out of her. She knows better than to run away to keep from giving valuable evidence—even evidence about a murder, which I know must have revolted her sense of the fitness of things."

"You mean the fitness of Parchly Heights."

Mayhew's grim mouth twitched. "If you'll promise not to feel too sorry for her I'll run her in on a charge of concealing evidence. Maybe even compounding a felony; it would stand."

For just an instant Miss Rachel, remembering Miss Jennifer's gaunt fright and despair, felt touched with pity. Then she remembered other things: a shabby woman who was dead because a murderer hadn't been caught quickly enough. A lonely yellow dog who had licked blood from his paws under a hydrangea bush and had gone away because his mistress was past loving or wanting him any more. A wedding ring whose putting on had been the signal and distraction for butchery. Remembering these things, Miss Rachel grew a little warm.

"Frighten her all you wish," she told Mayhew. "If it will help I'll come and make faces through the bars at her."

"You're all for law and order," he said curiously, looking at her.

"I'm for being human," she answered. "This murderer hasn't been."

"His killing Mrs. Terrice seems to be the thing you don't particularly like."

"It is." She touched his sleeve shyly. "Please go and talk to Pete and make him tell you why Addison was theatening him. I've a feeling that conversation was very important."

He raised his heavy brows. "And now hunches?"

"Hunches," she admitted.

"You think Pete is our murderer? How did he manage the trick with the bullet?"

"Your trick with the bullet will prove no trick at all once you know who really needed to kill Addison. Necessity is the mother of all sorts of inventions. . . . There was a necessity about Addison's dying. When you know it you'll find the invention."

He sighed at her and went away, though his brown bulk had a rebellious tightness.

Miss Rachel sat for a long minute on the stool of the dressing table; then she, too, went to the door and through it into the hall. She mounted the little dark rear stairs and looked in through Shirley's door. The room was empty. Miss Rachel went to the closet, to the pocket of the red robe where her treasures lay, and took them out.

There was the little box with its scarlet stripe, the bullet, and the bottle that had held paint thinner.

"I think that just now is the time," she said softly to herself, "to return each of these to its proper owner."

17

THAW'S DOOR was an oblong in darkness, the shabby knob bulging like an eye, a froth of dust showing at the sill. Miss Rachel knocked, and there was movement: a slow shuffling, like an animal in pain.

He looked out at her blindly. "Oh. Hello. Thought it might be Lee." His eyes searched the hall as if wanting his sister, wondering why she hadn't come. "I thought she'd—I thought we might be together."

"May I come in?" Miss Rachel asked, feeling like a white ghost in the gloom. "I've something for you."

He drew back. There was such tight, breath-held suffering in his face that Miss Rachel avoided looking at him. She tried not to think, too, of the forlorn woman who had kept the loyalty of her son. She waited until she was sure his attention was focused on her. "I have a little box I believe may have belonged to you."

She held it out, and the scarlet stripe made a bright band against her palm.

"Why, yes. Mother's ring." He took it slowly. "Look inside," she suggested.

"Inside?" He stumbled in prying up the lid, as though his

hands did something his mind was not upon. His chin was a hard line, and the little triangular scar stayed pale, like the imprint of a phantom hand. "There's nothing inside. Where's the ring?"

She waited a moment. "Your mother was wearing it."

"Was she?" He seemed puzzled.

"How long has it been," Miss Rachel asked, "since you were sure that your mother's ring was in your possession?"

His eyes held hers, and he seemed to feel his way toward an answer. "I don't know. I don't remember seeing it for quite a while. I kept it in the tray with my handkerchiefs." His eyes settled back of her, upon a large old-fashioned dresser. "Wait. It must have been there until a day or so ago. I'd have missed it before very long." Sudden curiosity sharpened him. "Where did you get it?"

"I found it in the hall," Miss Rachel said glibly. "Just lying there."

"In this upper hall?" he asked quickly.

"Yes."

"Someone took the ring out up here, then, and threw the box down and took the ring to Mother."

She didn't meet his probing stare. "I wouldn't know about that. I just thought you'd like your box back."

He crushed the frail cardboard in a sudden spasm and walked away and stared hard out through the window. "Thanks. I—I'm glad you brought it. I'd kept Mother's ring for her—she gave it to me when she went away. She put it in this box and asked me if I'd keep it safe for her. I knew what she meant. Someday, maybe, when Dad had got his fill of a pretty face and an empty head—" He broke off, choking. "I shouldn't say these things to you. I—I guess I'd better not talk any more."

The room grew still, and Miss Rachel, slipping out, kept the memory of his big frame against the light. She returned to Shirley's room, where she spent a surreptitious moment with a hanky in the closet. Then, brave again, she sallied out with the bullet.

Mr. Terrice's door was a mauve panel, and its crystal knob made a jewel. Miss Rachel rapped and waited, and there were brisk emotionless steps and then Mr. Terrice's face, shining glasses and cold eyes, looked out at her.

"What is it, Miss Murd?" he asked. He twiddled a pencil impatiently with one hand while he said it.

She opened her palm suddenly and let him see the bullet.

Just for a moment there was a flicker—fright, anger, or surprise—in his face. Then his heavy eyebrows made two arches of cool disinterest. "Where did you get that?" he asked.

"From where you put it," she said.

He paused, said carefully: "I'm afraid that I don't quite understand you."

"You put this into Shirley's closet, in the pocket of one of her garments. You made the mistake, though, of putting it into the pocket of a robe which your daughter had very recently given her. I'm afraid the police might think it had been there all the time. They might even think your daughter knew something about it."

He snatched at her hand with a movement as quick as a cat's, but she had put her hand behind her back.

There was a moment of watchfulness on her part and of strained self-control on Mr. Terrice's.

"What a ridiculous tale," he laughed. "How could you prove I'd put that bullet into Shirley's closet?"

"I saw you," she said helpfully. "You didn't know that I was watching, but I was. You looked around a bit and studied where it might most obviously be found. . . ."

He kept from throttling her with a visible effort. "I suggest you come inside, Miss Murd."

She backed a little farther into the hall. "I've wondered so often why you dislike Shirley so much. I can find nothing in the girl's make-up to account for the way you treat her. I think, therefore, that you must have disliked her mother—your step-sister—and that you're taking out that dislike on the child. You brought her here, too, because the servant problem was getting acute and Mrs. Terrice was not the housekeeping sort."

He opened the door quite wide in the manner of a conjurer showing a prospective victim that the cabinet had no hidden swords in it. "Please step in, Miss Murd. I won't approach you. I simply want to get at the bottom of the amazing in-accura-cies you have just displayed. I am not Shirley's enemy. Please come in."

She slipped past him and kept her eyes on the door while he pushed it almost shut.

"Now," he said, "you might begin at the beginning and tell me the complete story of this bullet."

"If you recall," she began, "your daughter Lee gave Shirley a red robe."

"A robe. I didn't know its color."

"This was to soften Shirley up so that she would turn over to you her stock in the Penny Novelties Company."

His face grew dark. "I could argue that point, but I suspect you have a deep prejudice on it. Go on about the bullet."

"Shirley took this robe to her room. This, you understand, was two days after Addison had been killed."

She waited and saw him grow still; saw one hand falter toward the knob, as though he suddenly wanted to be out into freer air.

"Two days—"

"Yes," she agreed, "two whole days. One would almost think that the bullet might have been put into the robe while it was still in Lee's room. I would, of course, if I hadn't seen you doing it."

He nodded, and the glasses shone with a reflection of light, but the eyes behind them were dead. There was suddenly no emotion in Mr. Terrice at all. "You saw me," he said. "You're sure of that?"

She looked at him wisely, with the pertness of a sparrow. "The time element," she said. "If there had been an immediate search made . . . Fortunately the police were lax about that."

He nodded, as though it made sense, as though it agreed with what he had been thinking.

"Good-by," Miss Rachel said suddenly. She put the bullet carefully on a desk. "And I wouldn't offer Shirley to the lieutenant again for a scapegoat. She doesn't quite fill the bill."

He said nothing but stood there and watched her go, and only at the last moment did his mouth twitch, as though a sudden thought had irked him.

Miss Rachel went back to Shirley's room and took her last treasure—the bottle which had held the paint thinner which had killed Shirley's little bird—and for long minutes she sat on the bed and thought. There was so much here to be careful about; it would be silly getting killed while one played at being a detective. With a last small sigh betraying her worry, Miss Rachel took the bottle and a length of ribbon and went down to the kitchen.

She found her cat on the outside porch, curled in a ball, an ear flickering now and then at the near approach of a bee.

Miss Rachel lifted the black head, and the green eyes slowly opened to show iridescent depths, like the shallow waters of a sea. A paw reached for her and two claws touched the taffeta sleeve and hung in it affectionately.

She tested the claws and found them sharp. "You're going to have to take care of yourself," she told Samantha. "Keep an eye out for whoever tries to take this bottle."

She tied the bottle to the string by its cap which contained the dropper, and then she looped the string about Samantha's throat and made a firm knot. The empty bottle was not heavy or large, but as Samantha rose to stretch it dangled against her breast and she regarded it angrily.

"Not here or now," Miss Rachel said, picking her up. "You're for lunch." She took the cat into the kitchen and shut her into the storage space under the sink.

Muffled yowls kept pace with her preparations of a cold plate, of a salad of marinated shrimp, avocado, and crisp cabbage. Shirley came to prepare the table. She had a frightened, wistful look.

"They've got Pete upstairs and he's shouting something over and over," she said worriedly. "It's something about Addison being a liar."

"Was he?" Miss Rachel wondered.

"Addison?" She considered. "No. He wasn't a liar. He was a drunkard and he'd let his clothes go and sometimes he—he didn't smell quite fresh. But I don't remember him lying. I don't believe that he did."

Miss Rachel kept a careful eye on her. "I've heard that Addison and Pete had an awful quarrel the day before Addison died. Something about you."

"About me? Whatever for?"

"Wasn't Pete jealous of the way Addison was acting?"

"How could he be?" She stood with the plates in her hands, staring. "I didn't like Addison at all, and Pete knew it. I hated the p-passes he made, and Pete knew that too. But he knew there wasn't anything serious, nothing I couldn't handle. And jealous—he wouldn't be that."

Miss Rachel turned a puzzled eye on the mixing of the salad. "Did Thaw ever show any interest?"

"He's—Thaw has been so full of his own misery since he came home from the Navy. I guess he just didn't know."

She turned in a hurry, so that Miss Rachel could not see her face, and went away through the pantry to set the table in the dining room. Miss Rachel garnished the cold plate and put dressing on the salad. She hummed over the making of a pot of tea, looked futilely for cake or some other dessert. One never knew, she thought irritatedly, from one meal to the next what would be at hand to prepare. Just how completely broke were the Terrices? From the looks of their kitchen, they were on the bitter edge. From the looks of Lydia's and Lee's wardrobes, they had money to burn. It occurred to Miss Rachel that the shortage might have become recent; that would account for the luxurious clothes bought a season before, explain the lack of groceries and the pretense of Lee's with the cologne bottles.

When Shirley returned they took in the salad and meats, and Miss Rachel poured the tea. Lydia came in on Mr. Terrice's arm, looking frail and beautiful in a slim gown of white lace on which the hysterics had left no slightest rumple. Or perhaps,

Miss Rachel thought, Lydia had hysterics only in old clothes or the nude.

This daring thought made her want to giggle, but the sight of Thaw's haunted eyes sobered her quickly enough.

"Excuse me, Dad, will you? I don't feel up to eating just yet."

Mr. Terrice nodded to him, went on to put Lydia into her chair.

Thaw, who had not come fully into the room, turned to Shirley, who was filling water glasses at the buffet. "Would you—could I talk to you for a little while? Outside somewhere. If you're having lunch now, too, I can wait. It's just"—he made an awkward, deprecating movement with one hand—"it's just an idea of mine. Maybe not a very bright one."

Mr. Terrice stared, and Lydia made her mouth look proper. But Shirley had turned on Thaw a pair of eyes full of moonlight and roses and the kind of adoration that makes the head swim. Thaw looked suddenly as though his had begun to swim and might keep right on.

Miss Rachel, slipping back to the kitchen, whispered to nobody: "So that's the way it is!" And she wished suddenly that Mr. Terrice's cold eyes and Lydia's prim ones might be blindfolded. People like that had no right to look at love.

She waited until she heard Lee's arrival and her plaint: "Cold cuts again? Can't we at least have a soufflé?"

Then she let the cat out from under the sink and made sure that the ribbon was secure and that the little bottle hung like a charm, shining against the black fur. Taking a plate of buns into the dining room, she felt the cat at her heels. A nervous feeling, like the march of a column of ants, went up her back.

She pushed the door from the pantry with her toe, and Samantha darted through and stopped there, tail twitching, eyes taking in and studying all of the Terrices and Shirley.

She mewed harshly in anger and then sat on her haunches and tried to claw away the torment of the dangling bottle.

"What on earth—?" said Lee.

Mr. Terrice said sharply: "Take it away, Shirley. We can't have a cat in the dining room. It's not sanitary."

Shirley bent down to pick Samantha up, and the cat struck at her, made a little jump, and howled.

Mrs. Terrice rose in the white lace and put a hand on either side of her plate and shut her eyes.

"She can't endure animals!" Lee cried.

Mrs. Terrice tried to turn away, to seek out the door to the living room. She put out a hand toward Mr. Terrice, who seemed not to see it because he was watching Shirley.

So Mrs. Terrice tottered a moment and then fainted. In the middle of a scream from Lee, and right into the salad.

18

"SHE RUINED it," Miss Rachel mourned to her cat as she un-knotted the ribbon in the kitchen. "She ruined it with her silly phobia about animals. Now I haven't any plan at all."

Samantha, free of the ribbon, sprang away and looked wist-fully at the door. Miss Rachel, letting her out, peeped through. Thaw and Shirley sat on a bench—the one she had occupied with Mayhew—and Shirley seemed terribly interested in a cab-bage near by, and Thaw was holding her hand and talking ear-nestly.

"I suppose he's making up for lost time," she thought happi-ly. She turned to find Mr. Terrice wrathful in the door to the pantry.

"Will you please dispose of the animal? Call the city pound and have it taken, or give it to someone. We can't have any such incident again." He read mutiny in Miss Rachel's glance, and his eyes flickered to the pile of luncheon dishes. "Well—ah—keep it out of the rest of the house, at any rate. If you don't mind fixing it too much—Mrs. Terrice will have a tray now, in her room."

Mrs. Terrice had been carried away by Thaw, frail in the

trailing lace, but Mr. Terrice and Lee had almost unconcernedly finished their meal.

His eyes searched about the kitchen, as if hunting the cat, and a faint line of worry etched a line between his brows. "Is it—? Wasn't there something tied about its neck?"

"A ribbon, I think," Miss Rachel said unconcernedly, getting a tray from the cupboard. "Blue, wasn't it?"

"I didn't notice," he said, withdrawing in somewhat of a hurry.

She chilled the salad in ice and made fresh tea and took it up the narrow back stairs to the second floor. Pete met her almost at the top step, plunging along with a bitter hump to his shoulders, blazing defiance in his face. He would have plunged past her to the stairs, but she fumbled awkwardly with the tray and seemed confused and about to drop it.

He paused to steady the tray in her hands.

"What's happened?" she asked. "You look angry. Very angry."

He drew back and rubbed a hand through the sandy tangle of hair. "I am angry. Clear through. The police are hounding me. They're trying to break up my—my friendship with Shirley."

"Do you love her very much?" she asked quietly.

His glance faltered away, and something undecided and secretive had come into his face. "Of course," he said. "Of course I do."

"And what makes you think the police are against you?"

"They're telling lies," he said hotly. "They're trying to prove we had something to do with Addison's getting killed."

"And you didn't?"

His eyes met hers frankly. "You know we didn't."

"What was it that Addison threatened to tell to Thaw?"

Incomprehension checked what he had been about to say. "Thaw? Addison didn't threaten to tell Thaw anything. Why should he?"

For no reason Miss Rachel suddenly believed him. "And Addison didn't say, during the course of that quarrel you had with him, 'What would Thaw say?'"

He studied for a long minute, the young face intent and the eyes searching. There was a look came over him then like a shutter closing, a masking of the mind from the face. He turned an expressionless gaze on her. "I don't think he said anything like that. I don't recall his having said it."

He ran past her and thudded down the stairs.

Miss Rachel struggled with an assortment of ideas. Pete hadn't recalled Addison's having threatened to tell Thaw anything, but the actual and verbatim remark had meant something to him. There was meaning, then, above and beyond a threat to talk to Thaw. "What would Thaw say?" She murmured it several times on the way to Mrs. Terrice's door.

Mrs. Terrice was lying down in a chiffon bed jacket and a tiny cap of pink marabou. It was quite the fluffiest and most youthful outfit for being ill in that Miss Rachel had ever seen— and Mrs. Terrice's face didn't match it. She had turned suddenly a great deal like the tired woman whom Miss Rachel had run into on the lawn. There were gaunt lines and shadows on her face, and the skin of the hand reaching for her tea was dry and sallow.

"I'm such a child," she whispered as Miss Rachel bent to place the tray. "Cats—any animal—frighten me so. And my nerves are on edge, anyway. Do you realize the position I'm in?"

Miss Rachel, thinking of the suspicion that marked everybody, said judiciously: "I just wouldn't worry about it."

"Not worry?" It was a fretful shriek. "Not worry—when I'm next in line for being killed?"

Miss Rachel simply stared.

Mrs. Terrice took a teacup and splattered tea on the snowy sheet and began to cry. "First my brother, poor drunken lovable brute. And then Lissa whom I—I'm afraid I wronged. And now, don't you see, *me?*"

Miss Rachel sopped at the tea with a napkin. "But why? Why you?"

"My family," she wept. "We're being wiped out. We're being murdered one by one for Addison's money."

"Then you won't have to worry," Miss Rachel comforted. "You're not getting it."

The handkerchief came away from the reddened eyes; the wet lashes flew wide. "Not—*getting it?* Really? You mean—someone else, first?"

"Lee," Miss Rachel said briskly. "Now dry your eyes and eat your lunch."

"Lee," Mrs. Terrice echoed blankly. She put an absent fork into the salad. "Was the will—or whatever it was—*recent,* do you think?"

"Not very recent, I believe," Miss Rachel said, considering that the information could do little harm.

"Do you think, then"—she was watching Miss Rachel curiously and attentively—"that Lee is in any danger?"

"I somehow don't think so." Miss Rachel refilled the teacup. "I think Miss Lee is quite safe for the time being."

Was there a brightening under the sallow misery of Mrs. Terrice? "You're not—not *suggesting*—?"

"That your stepdaughter did it? No. But someone did."

Mrs. Terrice took up a piece of shrimp and nibbled at it pensively. "If Lee did the—the crimes, then she'd be safe, wouldn't she? I'm just theorizing, of course; don't pay any attention to what I'm saying. But when murderers get what they want, then the murders *stop*, don't they?"

"Usually," Miss Rachel murmured, "unless it's turned into a habit."

Mrs. Terrice glanced at her sharply for any sign of fun. "Lee didn't like Addison. He spoiled things for her several times—parties going and he'd barge in drunk, things like that. Still, she'd have had to know that he was leaving a lot to Lissa and that Lissa was leaving everything to her. Otherwise, you see, it might not pay."

"Hardly," Miss Rachel agreed.

"And Lee loathed Lissa. She'd as soon have killed her as have swatted a fly."

"Odd, wasn't it, how little feeling she had for her mother?" Miss Rachel meditated. "One would think, almost, that she'd been brought up rather strangely."

Mrs. Terrice prodded a second shrimp as if displeased. "We trained Lee to love neatness and beauty, and she didn't find them in her mother. I don't suppose you ever saw Lissa alive." Her swift glance searched Miss Rachel's face. "She wasn't lovely at all, and she just kept getting shabbier and dirtier and less like a lady. It wasn't that she drank like Addison. I think her pride was gone. Simply gone entirely."

Miss Rachel, staring at the wall across the fluffy cap of marabou, studying the pastel water color of a French lady carrying a fan, said slowly: "Perhaps she was very lonely. Lonely and frustrated people often don't care for themselves as they should. There isn't any incentive to do so."

The bent head had become quite still. "I'm sure that I should try to keep as immaculate as possible, no matter what the circumstances. There are standards one simply can't ignore."

Miss Rachel murmured a perfunctory agreement and withdrew. She was apt to get a trifle warm when discussing Lissa Terrice; a prickling of anger annoyed her scalp when she thought of the vigil of the yellow dog.

She went up to Shirley's room and discarded the apron and put on a wrap. She spent some minutes going over the clothes in the closet and the dresser in a search for any new tamperings. Though she found nothing new of interest, she retained a feeling of vague worry as she went back to the lower floor.

In the second-floor hallway she thought she heard the faint click of a latch as she paused there to put on her gloves. She glanced without turning, saw a row of mauve panels and crystal knobs unmoving and innocent. She went down to the kitchen with the silly urge in the back of her mind to keep looking over her shoulder. Even a footfall on the stairs—after she'd reached the middle of the kitchen floor.

"I'm hearing ghosts," she scoffed to herself as she shut the cat under the sink so that she would not be followed. "I'll be seeing the cook's werewolf next. Fangs, tail, and all."

She went out into the bright sunlight and saw the bench empty where Shirley and Thaw had sat. She took the pathway to the alley in order to be as inconspicuous as possible. In less than ten minutes she was home.

The porch held that morning's newspaper, a bottle of milk, and a faint trace of dust that spoke of Mrs. Marble's absence. Miss Rachel took the key from under the mat and let herself in. The hall was cold and had an undefinably empty smell to it. Miss Rachel put down her bag and gloves and went to the letter box which opened from a slot on the porch.

Mr. Salter's rather startling handwriting—sea-gull tracks between astonishing capitals—stared at her from the top envelope. Miss Rachel tore the manila flap and took out the handkerchief which had been wrapped about Shirley's bird. She could see, now that Mr. Salter had pointed it out, that there was a fine black dust smudged into the cloth. This, then, would be gunpowder. She slid the handkerchief back into the envelope and went to the living room and sat down at her desk.

The room had a hollow, silent quality that was strange. Miss Rachel felt an uneasy chill until she placed the source of the impression: the clock had stopped. She went to the mantel and took the key and wound it, and then wished that she hadn't. The loud harsh ticking was worse, somehow, than the silence had been. It might, she thought unreasonably, keep her from hearing something else. She didn't wish to define what.

She sat down and put Mr. Salter's long official police envelope before her and took out a sheet of paper and began to write:

The Clue of the Man's Handkerchief
Found in her room by Shirley Grant and used by her to wrap her dead canary.
Proved by police analysis to contain grains of gunpowder.
No identifying initials or marks.
Shirley's impression that the handkerchief did not belong to Pete. However, Pete known to be in room during time bird was dying.
Conclusion: *One might reasonably suppose that the handkerchief had been used in connection with some tampering with a bullet. Perhaps the making of a live bullet out of a blank. From the streaks and smudges, it seems that the cloth was used to brush away the debris left from the job.*

After a good deal of sitting still and thinking, Miss Rachel went to the telephone in the hall and called the police laboratories. Mr. Salter, when she got him, was friendly as usual and as willing to help, except that he didn't know the ins and outs of bullets. Would she want the ballistics boys?

"I think so, yes. And thank you for sending the handkerchief."

"It wasn't anything. No connection, I suppose, between it and the Brill murder?"

"Oh, none," Miss Rachel put in in a hurry. No fury like Mayhew over evidence withheld. "None at all. I'm just dabbling."

Mr. Salter, after a remark about the strange antics that had come over Parchly Heights, let her talk to a man who stuttered.

The man who stuttered was Captain Leahy, and Miss Rachel, somewhat awestruck, realized that she was speaking with one of the foremost ballistics men in the United States.

"I'm doing some experiments, sort of"—she wondered what mad species of little old lady, in Captain Leahy's mind, could possibly do experiments with bullets—"and I was wondering if a blank cartridge, a pistol cartridge, could be made into a real shell that would kill somebody."

"W-w-we've been w-wondering the same thing, lady, and w-we've about decided it c-couldn't. Not by anybody sh-short of an expert. That answer your qu-question?"

"You're sure?" she pressed.

"Sh-sure I'm sure. A b-blank shoots wadding and c-carries only a small ch-charge of powder. How're you going to p-put a f-full charge and a steel j-jacket on that?"

"I see," she said quickly to sooth his impatience. "And thanks so much. I'm—I'm writing a mystery story."

"Oh." He laughed for no necessary reason that Miss Rachel could fathom. "Fine. S-send me a copy, w-won't you?"

She promised him a mythical book and hung up. "Now he's sure I'm crazy," she thought, going back to the desk.

The page about the clue of the pocket handkerchief stared up at her. She sat down to write the obvious conclusions.

The murderer had been experimenting with a bullet, most likely a blank which would fit Thaw's gun. The blanks were in Shirley's room, accessible to anyone. In returning the box of blanks, the handkerchief which had been used in wiping up the debris was dropped. Perhaps at this time, too, notice was first taken of Shirley's bird. The bird was drugged with paint thinner. As an experiment? Newspapers had printed accounts of a drunken man who had drunk some by mistake and almost died. Was the bird a sort of control? And didn't die quickly enough?

Without being conscious of where the thought had come from, she scribbled on another sheet:

Thaw was in the habit of bringing his mother into the house. Did he, by any chance, admit her on the day of the murder?

The idea was so startling, her conviction about it so sure, that she felt excitement tingle through her. If Thaw had admitted his mother, if some preparation for the murder had been in evidence and she had later grasped its significance . . .

There had been a sound—not a clock tick—from somewhere in the house, and she had missed it. A cold and sudden and belated realization struck her. She rose, and there was a footfall very soft and not far away.

And then her own black cat came to stand in the door and stare at her.

19

MISS RACHEL waited, feeling her own pulse thump in the silence, watching the faint movement of the cat's tail in the air. Once the cat glanced over her shoulder and mewed, and almost immediately after there came again the faint click of a door shutting.

Miss Rachel sat down suddenly because her legs were weak and her throat had turned dry from wanting to scream.

The impression she had felt on the stairs had been real, then, and she had been followed all of the way. Someone coming after her into the kitchen had paused to investigate the woes of Samantha and had inadvertently let out the cat. They had come here, the two of them, murderer and black following ghost. . . .

And for some reason the murderer had gone again.

She thought belatedly of the kitchen door and ran to it. There was no sign of anything unusual save the shaking of the leaves in the border of hollyhocks and a crushed place among the pansies.

She went back to her desk, where Samantha had installed herself among the letters, and ran through the remaining envelopes hurriedly. There were two advertisements—one for real estate and one for corsets—and a note about a food sale to be given by the Parchly Heights Ladies' Aid, and—at last—the impressive stationery of her bankers.

She ripped the thick white flap and took out the page.

The report inside was brief but enlightening. The bank, in the person of Mr. Toler, its vice-president, thought that Miss Rachel might do well to pick up some Penny Novelties stock if she could find it.

Penny Novelties, which had been begun as a hobby to manufacture toys, was now doing machine-gun and bombsight parts and its stock was soaring.

Miss Rachel, looking a bit grim, stuffed the bank's and Mr. Salter's envelopes into her purse and let Samantha follow her into the hall. Now she made sure that the old house was securely locked, both front and back, and removed the milk and the paper from the porch before setting out for the Terrices'.

She came up the back lawn, past the bench where Shirley had listened to Thaw's eager words, and onto the porch with a feeling of being watched. Who had followed her, she wondered, to her own home; had come in with a soft footfall and then gone away? And why?

In Shirley's room she found the girl mending linens.

Shirley read the banker's note with a puzzled look. "Does this mean I shouldn't lend the stock to Uncle John?"

Miss Rachel looked deeply into the wide, bewildered eyes. "Tell him first that you have learned its value. See then if he wants it."

"Will that prove something?"

"I think that it will." Miss Rachel took off coat and hat and gloves, put her purse with Mr. Salter's letter in it under the clothes in a drawer. She stood then a long moment deep in thought. When she turned to Shirley there was an expression of decision on her face. "I want you to tell Pete something too. I want you to tell him about the value of the stock. And to hint a little of what Thaw told you today."

Shirley's fingers, holding needle and thread again, trembled. "I could hardly tell him that. Thaw's different from what I thought he was. He's been wounded and confused, but he's going to be all right. I—I guess I'm in love with him too."

"Too?"

"You see," Shirley said miserably, "I've thought so long that I loved Pete and now I'm not sure."

"Will you do what I asked?" Miss Rachel pleaded. "If you do it will clear up a great many things."

"Are you sure?" Irrelevantly she added: "What do you think of Pete, really?"

"I'm afraid Pete is a bit devious," Miss Rachel answered. She evaded further questions by wrapping herself in the cook's apron and leaving the room. In the second-floor hall she turned and walked silently down the middle of the thick carpet.

"What would *I* do," she wondered abstractly, "if I were a murderer and I'd gotten nail polish off my victim and onto my clothes? I'd get the nail polish off as best I could, of course. Suppose I couldn't be sure . . ."

She listened with a pink ear at Mr. Terrice's door and, hearing no sound from within, she turned the knob and made an opening no wider than a pencil.

Still no sound, no movement. The cat rubbed her ankles and purred, and she made bold to open the door wide enough for Samantha to go through.

The cat sidled through willingly, and Miss Rachel took it for a sign of the room's emptiness and went in after her. Mr. Terrice's room was bright with sun, its heavy furniture gleaming, the windows thrown wide for air. Would Mr. Terrice be apt to be at work on the day of his first wife's murder? Miss Rachel thought not, but she recalled that Addison was to be buried today and that Mr. Terrice might have gone off to supervise details and to make ready the settling of Addison's estate. Nevertheless, she hurried.

She went rapidly through Mr. Terrice's desk, which seemed full of nothing but bills, the astonishing luxury of Lee's and Lydia's wardrobes being explained thereby. Many accounts had *Please Remit* stamped on them in red ink. In one note a grocer sadly informed Mr. Terrice that credit was being ended as of the date of the letter—more than a month before.

"Well," she thought, "he makes a salary, doesn't he? Why all the desperate shortage?"

She rummaged further.

She found a small ledger with entries in it as neat as Mr. Terrice's fringe of hair and shining glasses. From the ledger she discovered that Mr. Terrice made five hundred dollars a month in salary—less than she had supposed—and that his house payments were one hundred and fifty, and that Lee's sorority activities cost him a hundred more.

That left two hundred and fifty, of which one hundred was Lydia's allowance. Studying what became of the remainder: heat and lighting, repairs, cook's wages, lodge dues, and a dozen other items, Miss Rachel no longer wondered at the scanty and impromptu supply of food. The marvel was that there was any.

Mathematically Mr. Terrice was a conjurer. Miss Rachel looked further into his bag of tricks and came across the records of a disastrous venture into private brokerage.

All that he owed his former private clients was written down, and Miss Rachel blinked over the items. Miss Tabitha Fleck (poor timid mouse; Miss Rachel knew her) had been nicked to the tune of fourteen thousand dollars. And there were others, unfamiliar names and gross amounts that brought pink fury into Miss Rachel's small face.

She closed the desk on Mr. Terrice's bald robberies and went to his closet and worked at white heat. But though she found that Mr. Terrice did not stint himself on clothes and hung them up as meticulously as he wiped his spectacles, she found no trace of nail polish—half removed or otherwise.

She shook her skirts at the door, as if to shake off the taint of Mr. Terrice's hypocrisy, and crossed the hall to his wife.

Mrs. Terrice called, "Come in!" when Miss Rachel knocked. She was still in the bed jacket and the pink cap; she looked paler than ever—if that were possible—and flatter and thinner under the bedclothes. "Yes?" she murmured.

"Your tray," Miss Rachel said, poison-sweet. "And I might just straighten up a bit, too, while I'm here."

"Don't trouble yourself." She had shut her eyes, and the lids twitched and were blue.

"No trouble at all, I'm sure." Miss Rachel scurried about the room, setting it to rights. At the closet she paused. The billowing and fragile contents breathed sachet into the air, hung silken and shimmering in the gloom. Miss Rachel ran an experimental hand among velvet and chiffon, felt Mrs. Terrice's gaze between her shoulder blades.

"Don't touch my clothes, please. You might have something on your hand."

Miss Rachel, in an action purely involuntary, wiped the hand against the cook's apron, then turned scarlet with humiliation.

"My tray." There was a tinkle of silver and glass. "Will you take it now, please?"

Miss Rachel at the door felt that a curtsey was expected by the imperious woman on the bed, but she refused it. She went out ramrod straight and marched down to the kitchen.

She ignored the waiting dishes and stood thoughtful and looked out at the back yard. Mr. Terrice drove a blue sedan into the garage and came jauntily up the pathway; he paused once to brush at an invisible blemish on his trouser leg. When he came into the kitchen Miss Rachel was obediently at the sink. When the door to the pantry closed on him she dropped the soap as though it were hot.

"What nonsense to do dishes with a butcher loose among us," she snapped to herself. She wandered away into the laundry room and stared at the door to the cellar. This was the spot in which Pete had been busy with an iron, some repair work for Lee, during the time Addison had been killed.

She stole down a short stairs into gloom and dust, found herself facing a long littered bench on which were a vise and an emery wheel. She switched on the unshaded bulb above the bench for a better look. There was a furnace, shelves containing paint and nails and patching plaster and odds and ends of hardware. Miss Rachel read labels and whistled soundlessly to herself. Here was the source of many evils: paint thinner and luminous stuff which would have made the wolf's head and a lantern on the lens of which were painted deepening circles in green.

"Terror tonight, if I'm not mistaken," she whispered, and went back to the kitchen and worked furiously at the dishes until they were done.

After which she called Mayhew and made a rendezvous in

Mrs. Brenn's back garden at three and then went in search of Shirley.

Lee was with Shirley in the little room on the top floor. She was standing on a chair, slim in something new of black crepe made military with braid, and Shirley, with needle and thread, was putting a few stitches in at the hem.

Lee didn't deign to speak. She looked down critically and said, "I'm afraid you're getting it too low. I'm not an old lady, remember."

Shirley threw an apologetic glance at Miss Rachel and went on stitching.

Miss Rachel said pleasantly: "Your uncle is here, Shirley. I think it's time you showed him that letter."

Lee glanced at her curiously. "He's come to drive us to Addison's funeral. Ghastly, isn't it, that we have to sit through eulogies on that sot?"

Shirley flinched, and Miss Rachel went soberly to the bed and sat down.

"How long has it been," she asked, ignoring Lee's plaint, "since you saw anything of the werewolf?"

Lee stood still as death, but Shirley raised eyes full of innocence. "I didn't, you know. The cook saw him—it. And not even a real werewolf, then. The shadow."

"Standing by your door," Miss Rachel added.

"Waiting," Shirley put on, turning a little white. "I was foolish to think of it beyond the moment she spent telling me."

Miss Rachel seemed lost in abstraction; then: "Have you spoken to Pete as yet?"

Shirley said slowly: "Yes. He came past in the hall and I told him what you asked me to."

Miss Rachel studied the remaining nursery print. "How did he act?"

"Not in any particular way," Shirley said, biting a thread. "He stood awhile as though thinking something over and then went away."

Lee shook herself as if impatiently. "Hurry it, will you? Dad's waiting, if he's here."

"Shirley's going to see him," Miss Rachel said, getting up. "Give me that needle, child."

Miss Rachel, finishing the hem, managed to stick Lee Terrice quite nicely in the leg.

In Mrs. Brenn's back garden, where turnips made a show of green between splashes of sunflowers, Miss Rachel sat on an arbor bench and looked at the large form of Lieutenant Mayhew.

"I'm glad you're so big," she said. "It's such a comfort when trouble is in the offing. Like bulletproof armor, almost. You're too thick to let anything through."

"You're putting me up for gun bait," he said grimly, "and you just might, in advance, give me an idea what I'm dying for."

"We won't be dealing with murder tonight," she said. "We'll be working on my case. The tricks that were played on Shirley. I think that they'll be coming to an end."

"And just how will that help me in regard to the killing of Mr. Brill and the slaughter of his sister?"

"I don't know," she said simply. "Perhaps it won't help at all, except that it will clear away part of the deadwood and let you see the family more clearly."

He spent a moment staring at his shoes. "I saw Miss Jennifer. I took her to jail."

"Anything else?"

"The driver of the car who brought Addison home."

"What did they tell you?"

"That Addison was killed without anyone being near him. By the gun that was hidden in the niche. We knew it, anyway, but we needed witnesses. We're trying to trace the sale of the live shells that must have been bought to replace the blanks. There's a lot of work to be done before I'll know how that trick was worked in the den."

"Is—is Jennifer very frightened?"

His big face took on a look of pity. "You'll have to be kind to her for a long while. She's in a tank with the lowest. We hadn't a private cell for her."

"Let's don't worry about her now," Miss Rachel said simply. "There's so much to be done. The Terrices must have left now to see to Addison's burial. If you'll come with me I'll show you what I have in mind."

20

Miss Rachel waited, feeling her own pulse thump. The cat stirred against her ankles, ran claws into the covers, and growled faintly at the goblins of a dream. There was a gray glow from the sky outside: enough to show Shirley's figure curled and sleeping, the black frame of the bed, the closet door open, the slatternly chair against the wall.

Miss Rachel slid out upon the floor and put on a wrapper and went to the hall door and listened.

There had been light steps some minutes before; there now was silence.

Miss Rachel went out without a squeak of noise save a last-minute jump from Samantha, getting through the door with her, and slipped across to the cook's door and produced a key. It was a new key, made from a wax mold on the instructions of Lieutenant Mayhew. She slid it in and felt the bolt move. The ghostly confines of the cook's room opened before her.

She left the door open a slight way and went in and made a cautious circuit of the open space. The bed stood as it had, the wreath of garlic like a shadowy porthole on the wall above, the window on whose sill the little box had rested letting in the gray glow and showing Parchly Heights outside in the proper slumbers of midnight.

In a sudden fit of temper Miss Rachel climbed upon the bed and tore the garlic wreath from the wall. She took it to the window, raised the sash and unhooked the screen, and threw the garlic into the darkness below.

Then she went back to sit upon the bed.

The cat came with luminous eyes, slitted like a pixy's, and made mischief with the fringes of the old-fashioned spread.

The hall was a cavern of pitch-darkness, and the raised sash let into the room an erratic breath of cold air. Miss Rachel rubbed her shoulders, brushing away the chill. She wondered just how long she might have to wait before anything happened. If it did.

She began to think meanwhile of the preparations she and Mayhew had made and a telephone call she had put through without Mayhew's knowing. Tabby Fleck, she had recalled from school days, was timid under ordinary circumstances but inclined to rise up when others were downtrodden.

Miss Rachel had been careful in explaining the viewpoint of widows and orphans in regard to Mr. Terrice's activities.

Late before dinner Mr. Terrice had received a call. Scooting shamelessly upstairs to listen on the hall extension, Miss Rachel had heard Tabitha's wrath.

She hugged herself now in the dark, forgetting the cook's room and its ghost of ancient terrors, remembering Tabby's words and Mr. Terrice's choked replies.

The cat mewed softly and suddenly—not toward her but toward the hall. Miss Rachel, sobered and still, watched where the cat watched but saw nothing.

Then she thought that surely her eyes deceived her. There was a wavering pale spot on the panel of Shirley's door. The spot moved and grew bigger and was faintly green, like the reflection of an evil moon, and there began to inch across it a shadow.

Something tight and icy contracted Miss Rachel's muscles, and she threw an inadvertent glance toward the space occupied by the garlic wreath.

The shadow in the midst of green light grew until it was in focus and stood clear. Miss Rachel shut her eyes, then opened them at a sound from across the hall. There was a faint and steady rapping from the direction of Shirley's door.

Miss Rachel stared at the black shape of a crouching wolf. The rapping went on. The world was ice and inarticulate terror.

Shirley's door moved, drifted inward, and Shirley stood in the open space in a white gown, the tumbled dark hair about her throat, a bewildered look in her wide eyes. The edge of her gown was tainted with the green glow; the shadow of the crouching wolf seemed almost at her hand.

Miss Rachel ran to the window of the cook's room and took a match from her wrapper pocket and struck it quickly and let it flare close to the pane. Then she dropped it, stepped on it, began to run toward the hall as Shirley screamed.

Shirley was clinging to the door, her face gone wild with fear. Miss Rachel darted across to her and then jerked about to face the green light.

Big—an eye whose pupil was fanged terror—the green light hung at the far end of the hall, and against it stood the wolf, crouched, malevolent.

Shirley's sobbing breath went out on a long sigh, and she fell where she had stood and the green light sprayed her.

Miss Rachel put her slight strength to the task and dragged Shirley inside and to the bed. Big feet, more than one pair of them, pounded in the hall, and there was the crash of glass and loud cursing, and the green beam at the keyhole went out abruptly.

Miss Rachel put on the light and propped Shirley's feet up with pillows and let her head hang off the mattress. She looked small and disheveled in the huddle of white cotton gown, and paler than death itself could make her. Miss Rachel chafed her wrists, wrapped her well with blankets, prayed for a man to bring a bottle of whisky.

Thaw Terrice burst in wearing pajamas and a gently swelling left eye. He came to the blanket-wrapped figure and lifted it tenderly and crooned brokenly against the tumbled hair. Miss Rachel was about to tell him that fainted people should be left with their heads low and their heels high and then thought better of it. Perhaps Thaw's love was more practical, anyway.

He threw a single glance at her. "I woke up when Shirley screamed. What in hell was he doing to her?"

"Loving her, I suppose, in his way." Miss Rachel made haste to straighten the room, to adjust the dragged coverlets. And none too soon, for Mayhew's big-bear figure filled the door. "He wanted her to love him in return, you see," she said to Thaw, "and she didn't. She loved you, and he came gradually to see it."

"With better eyes than mine," Thaw said bitterly, hugging Shirley, who was rag-limp but now conscious. "I wish they'd let me really beat him."

"You landed one damned good one," Mayhew said, coming in holding the electric lantern Miss Rachel had seen in the cellar. On its green lens was the black-paper silhouette of a wolf. "He had a screen he diffused this with and made it large," Mayhew added. "And this Halloween tick-tack thing." He held out with the other hand a collection of strings and a stick, the sort of arrangement boys tap on windows with when mischief gets the better of them. Mayhew made a sound like a raspberry. "Kid stuff. Old-woman gossip about werewolves. Who'd swallow it?"

"It's easy to frighten a girl alone in the middle of the night. And he had the cook, of course, who believed in it to begin with."

"But why?" Shirley whispered.

Miss Rachel turned gentle eyes on her. "So that you would think one of the Terrices was persecuting you and would turn to him. And he needed the bolstering of your money to make the break here too. That's why I asked you to tell him today of the value of your stock—and that you were beginning to know that you loved Thaw. I knew then that Pete would make a supreme effort to terrify you."

Two uniformed officers came to the door, and Pete struggled between them, crimson and cursing. He avoided Shirley's gaze but looked on Miss Rachel with fury.

"I've suspected you from the beginning," she said.

He tried to spit at her and was slapped in the mouth for it and dragged below.

"Are you keeping a watch on the garage?" Miss Rachel asked softly.

"We are that—" Mayhew began, and stopped as the roar of a motor rent the night air and then subsided.

She ran with him, her light tap echoing his heavy thud. Shirley and Thaw needed only each other now, love's balm being a magic thing, and she didn't like looking at Pete. The night air was cold and the grass slippery with dew. There were lights in the Terrice garage and two dark bodies battling on the cement ramp to the alley. The light showed brass buttons and serge on one man, and Mr. Terrice's thoroughly broken glasses hung off the ear of the other.

"Did just what you said he'd do," Mayhew yelled, pitching in.

"Tabitha's committee," Miss Rachel explained, though Mayhew didn't hear. "They're calling on him in the morning. It was now or never."

She stopped where a small black bag lay tilted on the ramp and stirred it with her toe so that its broken latch faced the light. Stuffed inside were sheaves of bonds. "Addison's, of course," she whispered. "All that he could rifle before the accounting had to be made."

She took the satchel away into the house and let a uniformed policeman keep it for her. She went then by way of the music room and the golden grillwork and peeped in at the living room. Pete was here, defiant on a frail chair whose satin back made his old cords look disreputable. An officer near by was staring at the pastel furnishings as if he wanted to eat them.

Mrs. Terrice came in hesitantly. "I'm wanted here? Someone rapped at my door and said I should come down. Where is everyone? Pete, what is it?"

He growled at her and kept his head turned.

She was wearing a crepe negligee the exact color of a lilac blossom. Two little shoes of white fur peeped out as she sat down on one of the sofas which faced each other from either side of the fireplace. The uniformed man had risen at her entrance, looked blank at her questions, and now sat down again. She gave him a weary smile. "It's frightening, being routed out in the middle of the night. Are you sure I'm wanted?"

"I guess so," he said.

"I'm Mrs. Terrice."

"Pleased to meet you, ma'am."

She looked away as though he disappointed her; at that moment Lee came in in a long tailored robe of blue.

Lee was furious. Her eyes burned, and the rope of yellow hair shook with the energy of her speech. "Dammit, I won't be rounded up like cattle! Where's Father? Why isn't he here, giving these brutes a piece of his mind? Pete"—she turned on him like a snake—"what's happened to you? Have you been arrested?"

Pete said nothing; his stare was stone.

"You have been arrested," Lee said slowly, some of her anger dying. "They've caught you for killing Addison and Lissa."

Mrs. Terrice gave a whimpering cry. The corner of Pete's mouth twitched and was still. His eyes never wavered.

Shirley came in with Thaw at her elbow, but there was little time for Mrs. Terrice and Lee to grasp the feeling between them, for Mr. Terrice made, at that point, an entrance more abject than even Miss Rachel could have wished for him.

In the confusion Miss Rachel slipped around the grille and seated herself inconspicuously on a chair near the stairs. No one saw her. They were looking at Mr. Terrice, a handcuffed Mr. Terrice who lagged, broken and cringing, between two victorious policemen. One was Mayhew. He looked like a bear that has just bagged the honeypot.

Mr. Terrice sank into the nearest chair he could find. He looked once and very briefly at Mrs. Terrice, and she cried: "John! However could you! My own brother, and Lissa."

And very oddly, for he was so openly finished and disgraced, Mr. Terrice grinned. Grinned and relaxed. And Miss Rachel suspected that no one had seen that, either.

Mayhew straightened his clothes—victory had been a strenuous affair—and fished forth his battered notebook and a pencil which looked as though it had been chewed. "I'll take down anything you have to say. You might as well talk and get it over with."

Pete looked across the open space, where Shirley sat in her red robe with Thaw's hand on her arm. "I'm damned if I know why I did it. I could have got a job and got out that way, I guess. Put it down to my moron's instinct for going at things the hard way."

"What's he talking about?" Lee cried.

"The tricks that were played on Shirley," Thaw put in. "Your shoes, and the broken stuff, and that werewolf scare the cook was screaming over. It was all a gag to win Shirley and get her to go away with him."

"But, Pete," Shirley asked, "why didn't you just say something? Tell me how you felt, and—"

"I don't know," Pete said disgustedly. "I thought you'd just naturally bring it up yourself when you were tired enough of the gaff."

"And my little bird," she said quietly. "Did you have to do that?"

"I didn't do it," he said. "Believe me just this once, Shirley. I didn't hurt your bird."

She flushed but went on evenly: "I don't believe you, Pete. Killing my little bird was part of the mischief, and you admit doing that."

"And the werewolf carries over into murder," Mayhew said grimly. "There was an attempt to make it seem as though. Lissa Terrice was killed by one of the things—footprints, stuff like that."

A look of slow realization had come over Pete. "Wait. Hell, I didn't even know the woman. How could I kill her? *Why* would I?"

Miss Rachel stood up with a rustle of taffeta and came to a point where she was in a better position to talk to Mayhew. "Much as I hate to save Pete's neck for him, I'm afraid I shall have to. He didn't, Shirley, kill your little bird. He played tricks with things you were supposed to have broken and damaged— Addison was onto that part of it, and they had a quarrel about it—and he performed the silly tricks with the werewolf motif after, probably, the cook had given him the idea with her superstitions."

Pete nodded with a grudging motion.

"Addison's remark which Lee overheard: 'What would Thaw say?' was really, I think, 'What would the law say?' Which makes more sense, as some of the articles Pete ruined were valuable."

Pete had turned sullen at mention of Addison's name, but again he nodded agreement to what Miss Rachel had said.

"But Pete's antics end there," Miss Rachel went on. "He wanted you to need him and to go away, especially after he discovered that you might have enough money to finance the departure. He didn't kill your bird. The murderer did that as an experiment in dying. Other experiments had included taking apart a blank shell and trying to make a live bullet out of it. In wiping up the mess the murderer had used a man's cheap cotton handkerchief, which was dropped in your room and which you used to wrap the dead bird in before you brought it to me."

From her robe pocket Miss Rachel produced the handkerchief, which Mayhew took grimly in his own hand to stare at.

"The handkerchief, I think, is Thaw's. It doesn't quite match the quality of Mr. Terrice's."

A sudden and electric silence had come over them all. "There has been, you see, from the beginning, a deliberate attempt to cast guilt upon other people. The murderer has used every-one's tools save his own. Thaw's gun, Lee's nail-enamel solvent, the pocket of Lee's robe for an extra bullet to hide for suspi-cion's sake, the cook's room for implements not yet needed for crime. . . ."

Mayhew had his eye on Mr. Terrice, an almost somnolent Mr. Terrice who watched Miss Rachel as a critic might watch an especially boring play.

"Then you," Mayhew began, putting a big finger on John Terrice's shoulder, "you're the—"

"Just one thing more," Miss Rachel interrupted. "I'm sure that the murderer wore the right garments in the murder of Mrs. Terrice—Lissa Terrice. I can't find any trace of a stain made by nail enamel in the closets of Lee or Mr. Terrice or Shirley. Thaw I omit because I'm sure he genuinely loved his mother, and Pete I exclude for lack of motive. I suggest, therefore, that you look in Mrs. Terrice's clothes for the thing you want."

21

Mrs. Terrice, for an instant startled, gave an odd cry of rage. "How dare you!" She sat somewhat more erect. "How dare you accuse me—in my own home—of the murder of my brother and sister?"

Mayhew and a uniformed man had disappeared. Miss Rachel, watching their going, said slowly: "A profitable pair of crimes, since Lee is under your influence and her having her mother's money would be, for all practical purposes, the same as your having it."

Mrs. Terrice looked bewilderedly at the others, as if asking them what on earth had come over this old lady, and Lee cried: "Shut up! Don't dare say such things."

Mr. Terrice spoke for the first time. He said very coldly: "A bullet—the sort of bullet that killed Addison—was put into the pocket of a robe hanging in your closet. It was a decoy, Lee, to get you into trouble."

Lee and her father stared at each other, as though some thought common to them both had come into full flower at the same moment.

"No," Lee whispered. "I've—I've always loved her so."

Mrs. Terrice put out a frail silky hand. "Lee dear—" And then she was still—still and quite pale—watching Mayhew's return. Mayhew carried a black ball of chiffon.

"Is it yours?" he asked. The thing unrolled and hung there limply, and on the gossamer skirt was a great place rubbed awry.

"Never go murdering in chiffon," Miss Rachel thought. "It won't stand cleaning afterward."

Mrs. Terrice stood up. She looked at Lee, at the horror in Lee's eyes, and said lightly: "I suppose you've loved the wrong woman all these years. Lissa was squeamish about demanding money. I'm not. I'd get it somehow."

Mr. Terrice chuckled and kicked the bag which had been put near him. "Not from me, you won't. I've cheated my last client, Lydia. Silks and satins come too high. I should have stayed with calico."

For just a moment Mrs. Terrice looked as she must have looked when she killed her brother and Lissa. A ghastly and furious hatred looked out of her eyes. "I know what you have done," she said.

"Do you?" he grinned.

"But what about my mother?" Thaw cried. "Addison—you hated him. But Lissa had never done you any harm."

"She knew about the bullet," Mrs. Terrice said dully. "Somehow she knew." The eyes that had held fury and resentment were burned out. "And she died without telling me *how* she knew." Mrs. Terrice suddenly covered her face with her hands.

Miss Rachel said: "You were in the habit of bringing your mother here, Thaw. Did you bring her in shortly before the murder?"

He stared back numbly. "Yes. I lied before, in some twisted idea of trying to protect her memory. I did bring her here. We talked in the den, and Mother walked about and spoke bitterly of the past, and several times she touched different things—things she'd had in the old home—and she was crying."

"And the desk was one of the things she touched?"

"It was." His eyes brooded over the hurtful memory. "She ran her fingers over the drawers and the edges of the top."

"And felt there, no doubt, the bullet you had concealed in preparation for killing Addison." Miss Rachel had turned to Lydia, fallen wide-eyed on the broad couch whose colors had been meant to complement her beauty. "Was it gum, paste—some such thing?"

"A bit of wax," Lydia said quietly.

"And after Addison's murder she told you of what she had felt there under the edge of the desk?"

Mrs. Terrice made no answer. She let the silence increase in the room, felt no doubt the sardonic stare of Mr. Terrice and the broken and incredulous look on Lee. "You all think that I'm crazy, don't you?" she asked suddenly. "I'm not. I've loved beauty and order all of my life, and I intend to keep having them. Even now." And she took, with startling swiftness, a tiny knife from the bosom of the lilac negligee.

Shirley's scream, Thaw's bitter cry came just at the moment that Mrs. Terrice plunged her little dagger home.

But Mr. Terrice remained cool, and after a while Miss Rachel saw that he was taking a pair of extra spectacles from a case and was polishing them thoroughly.

They walked through the last of the moonlight, the big detective and the little old lady who trotted sometimes to keep up with his giant stride.

"If you knew, why didn't you tell me?" He kicked at a flowering shrub that touched the sidewalk. "If you guessed that the tricks with Shirley and the murders were two different and distinct businesses, you might have let me know."

"I thought for a long while that Pete was working on Shirley. He had the obvious motive of wanting to alienate her from the Terrices. As for the crimes—we couldn't have solved them without Mr. Terrice."

"I didn't notice any startling co-operation on his part," Mayhew complained. "What did he do?"

"Once I convinced him that the murderer was trying to implicate Lee—his favorite child, obviously—he very nicely planted that chiffon robe in Mrs. Terrice's closet for you to find. He thought he'd be slipping away with what he could get out of Addison's property, of course, the loose bonds and negotiable things that couldn't be traced. But nevertheless, we owe him a lot."

Mayhew had paused; he was a large and angry shape under the moon. "Wait. How do you know he planted that robe?"

"It wasn't present when I glanced through her clothes today. She'd hidden it—Mr. Terrice can doubtless tell you where, if you want to bother to get it out of him. She hid it after the removal of Lissa's nail enamel hadn't been entirely successful and after she'd emptied Lee's bottle of polish remover trying to do it."

"How did you arrive at that conclusion?"

"Because, you see," Miss Rachel said earnestly, "Lissa's murder was so obviously a woman's crime. All the details of it—the decoy wedding ring, the vengeful butchery, the letting in of the dog to see his murdered mistress—I hate that touch—and the attempted removal of the nail enamel: these were all the acts of a weak and jealous person. Who should be jealous of Lissa but her sister Lydia, who seemed on the surface to have everything and yet actually had nothing? Whose debts were becoming heartbreaking, whose husband was on the verge of leaving—she'd sense that—and whose hollow vanity was on the edge of staring at itself in the mirror of old age?"

"And you think Mr. Terrice knew all of this? All the details of the murder?"

"No. I think he was at first genuine, though nasty, about suspecting Shirley. Then the matter of the bullet planted on Lee stirred him up. I—I set some of his clients on him, too, just to spur him a little. I knew if he had to clear out to save himself financially he'd want to leave something to make life unpleasant for the guilty one—providing he knew who it was. He must have searched like mad to find that robe and been sly to get past Lydia to plant it in her closet."

"We'd have gotten her without this hocus-pocus," Mayhew grumbled. "We'd found the store that sold her the bullets. The owner was coming out to identify her the first thing in the morning. You didn't have to—"

"I know," she admitted meekly. "I don't have to. I even deserve the frights I get—such as Mrs. Terrice following me today to murder me for being a meddling old woman. The cat rushed in in front of her, and she's genuinely afraid of them and had a shock and had to go back home."

Mayhew walked on in silence, stopped at last with her before the high porch of her house. "I won't scold you any more. I heard Shirley promising you a flower out of her bride's bouquet. I suppose that goes into your memory book."

She touched his sleeve shyly in the dark. "Keep an eye on the dogs in the animal shelter, will you? If the yellow dog shows up I'll take him."

"More souvenirs," Mayhew grumbled. "Let me warn you about Miss Jennifer. She's apt to give you a souvenir you're not looking for."

Miss Rachel looked up to the lighted windows of the living room and sighed. "I might as well go in and face it. If she's too angry I might have to go to a hotel. Good night."

She went softly up the stairs, the cat drifting after her like a shadow, and Mayhew grinned suddenly and turned away.

The hall was dim, but the living-room lamp shone on Miss Jennifer's snapping eyes and face white with suppressed emotion.

There was a long, painful moment of silence.

Miss Rachel spoke from a dry throat. "Jennifer! Can you find it in your heart to for—?"

"Come in and sit down, Rachel," Miss Jennifer said ominously.

Miss Rachel slid in upon a chair. She wanted to run; she wanted to weep; she wanted to do anything but face the terrible dark intentness of poor Jennifer's eyes, fresh from the horrors of the city jail.

"Be quiet," Miss Jennifer said strangely, "while I tell you about it. I hardly know where to begin. Things were confused at first. There's a place called a tank, only it isn't, really."

Miss Rachel visioned a round frightfulness made of steel. "And the people inside—"

"Wretches," Miss Rachel thought, "poor wretches, derelicts, beaten things. . ."

"I'm telling it all wrong," Miss Jennifer decided. "But that jail, Rachel! You wouldn't believe, but it's full—just absolutely full—of the *most fascinating people!*"

Miss Rachel stammered: "And you—"

"And I had," Miss Jennifer rushed on, "the most wonderfully exciting time!"

THE END

DISCUSSION QUESTIONS

- What kind of sleuth is Rachel Murdock? Are there any traits that make her particularly effective?

- Were you able to predict any part of the solution to the case?

- After learning the solution, were there any clues you realized you had missed?

- Would the story be different if it were set in the present day? If so, how?

- Did the social context of the time play a role in the narrative? If so, how?

- What role did the geographical setting play in the narrative? Would the story have been different if it were set someplace else?

- If you were one of the main characters, would you have acted differently at any point in the story?

- Did you identify with any of the characters? If so, which?

- Did this story remind you of any other books you've read?

MORE DOLORES HITCHENS FROM
AMERICAN MYSTERY CLASSICS

Read on for a preview of
another case for Rachel Murdock in
The Alarm of the Black Cat,
available now in hardcover,
paperback, and eBook

CHAPTER ONE

THERE ARE times when Miss Rachel Murdock considers that the solution of murders should be left to the general public.

More specifically, she remembers the case which she has pleased to call the Affair of the Little Meannesses. By Little Meannesses she refers to a number of things which to the official mind might have meant nothing: the burying of glass in the path of an old woman's fingers, the shutting in of a cat, the spoiling of a swing, and the death of a toad.

It was the toad, in the role of innocent bystander, who first savored the particularly brutal kind of death which hovered over the four houses at the end of Beecher and Chatham streets. The toad, drowsy in the heat of the underside of a rosebush, looked up to meet the face of Murder, and he died as befits a gentleman, quietly and without too much struggle. Perhaps he knew at that moment, by some divine dispensation, that his dying lessened and relieved, though only temporarily, the stored hatred which was soon to infect the neighborhood. But this is fancy; the heel which had mangled the toad, after wiping itself on the turf, walked away with a new caution, so that perhaps the murder of the toad had best be chalked up to practice.

The toad was eventually found by the little girl who had been in the habit of feeding him flies; he was wept over, wrapped in tissue paper, and put into a shoe box for decent burial. But between prayer and covering, between the last look of love and the first odor of dissolution, Miss Rachel saw him, and so he had not died in vain.

Whether Miss Rachel had any business being at the end of Beecher Street is a matter for debate, but the necessity for her seeing the toad is above question.

Miss Rachel will say that she happened to be at the end of Beecher Street because she needed to rent a house. This is a rank untruth; Miss Rachel owns a house in which she has lived these many years with her sister Jennifer. The fact is that at the age of seventy Miss Rachel has become restless with a desire for travel. She has discovered that one of the cheapest and most comfortable modes of travel in and about Los Angeles and Hollywood is by means of a rental agent's automobile. The question of the cost of gasoline and oil has never worried her. To Jennifer's fret about the ethics of letting rental agents cart her about to numberless houses which she had no intention of renting, Miss Rachel makes the simple reply that she did actually rent a house.

For a month, Miss Jennifer sniffs.

This remark always rouses in Miss Rachel a mild wonder that so few days could contain so much mystery and creeping, relentless horror. That the little toad, dead in his cardboard coffin, could have been the forerunner of days of blood, nights of fear, and hours when Miss Rachel peeped from under her blinds with a core of terror inside her drawn tight as a fiddlestring. That the month of September, slipping off the calendar, marked the end of an eternity of watchfulness, a lifetime of breath-stopping dread.

She sometimes wonders what the net result might have been if she had never seen Mr. Toad at all.

The rental agent was a round, smooth little man dressed in a bright blue suit and possessed with a determination to please. His car was a sedan, almost new, and he drove it well; so well that Miss Rachel allowed him a second day of her time. It was on this second day that he took her to the vacant house at the end of Beecher Street.

Beecher Street begins with the dwindlings of an outlying shopping district in Los Angeles; it climbs hill of flats and scattered shops; it descends into a valley of old mansions and a park; it keeps bravely paved onward through an empty subdivision, and it ends on a grassy flat beyond which rise the blue Santa Monica foothills. It was in the shadow of these foothills, late in the afternoon, that Miss Rachel stepped from the rental agent's car to inspect a house.

It was a gray house built in the style of 1910, two-storied, with a big front porch, bulging windows, much latticework and trimmings. The garden was gone to weeds. The gate squeaked. On either side were two other houses, one white and one brown, with gardens well kept and with a look of having been long lived in.

Miss Rachel smoothed her taffeta skirt away from the reach of a nail in the gatepost, went up the path with the agent following, and stood on the porch while he inspected his keys.

The front door opened upon gloom and an odor of old wallpaper.

The agent said, "This isn't at all new, of course, but it's very reasonable. Thirty-five a month. Might be had for thirty, providing you'd sign a lease for it." He tried to pierce the placid expression of Miss Rachel's face for any interest she might feel. "Would you perhaps like to see the rooms?"

Miss Rachel, having in mind a good view of the hills with the sun going down behind them, suggested starting with the upstairs, rear. The puzzled little man preceded her, opened doors, and made a rambling sales talk. He by now considered Miss Rachel mildly eccentric, though she was still classified in his mind as the sweet-old-lady type, and he liked the way she smelled of lavender.

Miss Rachel looked for the hills through a sparkling pane. What she discovered was the little girl burying her toad.

"It's a very private neighborhood," the agent pointed out. "You'll notice there are just these four houses on the entire block. No traffic. The street ends just below."

"Mmmmmm," said Miss Rachel.

The little girl was saying a prayer over the open grave. She had her eyes shut tight and her grubby hands pressed up under her chin.

It occurred to Miss Rachel that this particular window was exceptionally clean, considering the state of the rest of the house. She drew back a little. Faint in the dust that covered the floor were a man's footprints. Round blobs of wax, perhaps a dozen, decorated the sill and the floor. A circular imprint marked the center of the sill. But most odd of all was a scattering of cake crumbs which Miss Rachel, testing surreptitiously between her fingers, found fresh and moist.

Through the window she had an excellent view of the two back yards on either side and of the house across the weed-grown alley whose rear door faced her.

On the back porch stood a woman, heavy of body, whose face shone out of the dusk and seemed to contemplate the little girl.

In its Slavic simplicity Miss Rachel could read no expression whatever, but there was an air of watchfulness in the way she held her head. The little girl had begun to slide the box down into the hole she had made for it. Miss Rachel was possessed with a sudden desire to know what it was she was burying in the yard below.

The agent was busy pointing out the excellent condition of the doorknob, since he had heard that most elderly women lock themselves into their rooms at night. Miss Rachel brushed past.

"There are four bedrooms up here," he said quickly, going after. "The right front is the biggest, very lovely; the paper's in fine condition, and the . . . ah . . ."

Miss Rachel was tripping downstairs.

He followed with a sigh, resigning himself to not renting the house and wondering what his wife might be having for dinner. To his surprise Miss Rachel did not make for the front door. At the foot of the stairs she turned right toward the kitchen. He stared after her and heard the snap of the back-door latch and the squeak of a hinge as she went out.

In the weedy garden Miss Rachel walked with caution, fearing to alarm the child; when the little girl looked up Miss Rachel smiled.

The little girl did not smile back; the blue eyes were grave and the round chin very much under control.

"You have a pretty box," Miss Rachel said tactfully. "It seems a shame to put it in the ground."

The little girl put down a hand and smoothed the box lid gently. "My toadie's inside. I'm burying him because he's dead."

Miss Rachel's zeal went out with a quick flow. Whatever she had expected from the array of footprints in the empty house, the watching woman, the little girl with her box, it had not been the mere burial of a toad.

"This was his garden," the child went on quietly, "and he took care of the rosebushes when nobody else wanted them. Sometimes he let me feed him a little—flies, you know—and he wasn't afraid any more if I came up careful." She lifted the lid of the box, peeked in at the tissue paper, her face averted lest Miss Rachel catch a glimpse of tears. "I loved him, and now he's all mashed."

The juxtaposition of love and destruction caught Miss Rachel's thought, and she bent over. The child glanced at her quickly, as if to see whether the delicate little old lady were making fun. Some idea of Miss Rachel's sympathy reached her; she took the lid off the box and unfolded the tissue paper.

No look of revulsion marred Miss Rachel's countenance. She inspected the broken toad and saw that the creature's head was marked at one spot with what might have been the corner of a heel. The green skin gave evidences of trampling: soil and twigs and bits of leaf mold. The watery eyes looked serenely at nothing.

"I think he's gone to heaven now, don't you?" The little girl took anxious care with the fitting of the box lid. "He was nice; he was always here waiting when I wanted to play. He didn't bite or scratch, either."

"I think he's gone there," Miss Rachel agreed. She watched while the little girl covered the box and patted the earth to firmness. She judged the child to be about eight. Her clothes and hair and skin spoke of care and good taste. Her pink print dress was hemmed now with dust, but it must have been immaculate before the burial of the toad.

The child sat frowning for a moment; her light brows made

a tangle where they met like a little mingling of feathers. "You know, I'd better mark this, hadn't I? I wouldn't want to forget. When the roses come again it would be nice to put a bouquet here." She inspected Miss Rachel as if for signs of disagreement.

"That's a sensible idea," Miss Rachel said. "Why not find a nice smooth stone and mark his name on it?"

The little girl looked about, stood up uncertainly. "I'll help you look for one," Miss Rachel went on.

"Oh. Would you?"

Miss Rachel began to search the ground and if she saw the puzzled face of the rental agent looking at her through the glass panel of the rear door, she gave no sign. Under a rosebush she found what she had sought, Mr. Toad's field of honor. She bent over and raked at the leaf mold with a thin, delicate hand and found heavy heel marks which had overlapped each other in the making. The heel was that of a man's shoe or of a woman's stout oxford. Remembering the condition of the toad, Miss Rachel had a sudden vision of fury and a chill.

She raised her head. The sky above was the clear luminous blue of after-sunset, the Santa Monica mountains a brown line to the north with a row of trees like a cockatoo's crest going up to the summit. In the high clear air a flock of swallows shone with reflected gold.

But the earth was darkening with a foretaste of night. Under the rosebushes lay the shadowy beginnings of twilight, and a stone which the little girl had found showed bone-white against the dusky earth.

All titles are available in hardcover and in trade paperback.

Order from your favorite bookstore or from
The Mysterious Bookshop, 58 Warren Street, New York, N.Y. 10007
(www.mysteriousbookshop.com).

Charlotte Armstrong, *The Chocolate Cobweb.* When Amanda Garth was born, a mix-up caused the hospital to briefly hand her over to the prestigious Garrison family instead of to her birth parents. The error was quickly fixed, Amanda was never told, and the secret was forgotten for twenty-three years . . . until her aunt revealed it in casual conversation. But what if the initial switch never actually occurred? **Introduction by A. J. Finn.**

Charlotte Armstrong, *The Unsuspected.* First published in 1946, this suspenseful novel opens with a young woman who has ostensibly hanged herself, leaving a suicide note. Her friend doesn't believe it and begins an investigation that puts her own life in jeopardy. It was filmed in 1947 by Warner Brothers, starring Claude Rains and Joan Caulfield. **Introduction by Otto Penzler.**

Anthony Boucher, *The Case of the Baker Street Irregulars.* When a studio announces a new hard-boiled Sherlock Holmes film, the Baker Street Irregulars begin a campaign to discredit it. Attempting to mollify them, the producers invite members to the set, where threats are received, each referring to one of the original Holmes tales, followed by murder. Fortunately, the amateur sleuths use Holmesian lessons to solve the crime. **Introduction by Otto Penzler.**

Anthony Boucher, *Rocket to the Morgue.* Hilary Foulkes has made so many enemies that it is difficult to speculate who was responsible for stabbing him nearly to death in a room with only one door through which no one was seen entering or leaving. This classic locked room mystery is populated by such thinly disguised science fiction legends as Robert Heinlein, L. Ron Hubbard, and John W. Campbell. **Introduction by F. Paul Wilson.**

Fredric Brown, *The Fabulous Clipjoint.* Brown's outstanding mystery won an Edgar as the best first novel of the year (1947). When Wallace Hunter is found dead in an alley after a long night of drinking, the police don't really care. But his teenage son Ed and his uncle Am, the carnival worker, are convinced that some things don't add up and the crime isn't what it seems. **Introduction by Lawrence Block.**

John Dickson Carr, *The Crooked Hinge.* Selected by a group of mystery experts as one of the 15 best impossible crime novels ever written, this is one of Gideon Fell's greatest challenges. Estranged from his family for 25 years, Sir John Farnleigh returns to England from America to claim his inheritance but another person turns up claiming that he can prove he is the real Sir John. Inevitably, one of them is murdered. **Introduction by Charles Todd.**

John Dickson Carr, *The Eight of Swords.* When Gideon Fell arrives at a crime scene, it appears to be straightforward enough. A man has been shot to death in an unlocked room and the likely perpetrator was a recent visitor. But Fell discovers inconsistencies and his investigations are complicated by an apparent poltergeist, some American gangsters, and two meddling amateur sleuths. **Introduction by Otto Penzler.**

John Dickson Carr, *The Mad Hatter Mystery.* A prankster has been stealing top hats all around London. Gideon Fell suspects that the same person may be responsible for the theft of a manuscript of a long-lost story by Edgar Allan Poe. The hats reappear in unexpected but conspicuous places but, when one is found on the head of a corpse by the Tower of London, it is evident that the thefts are more than pranks. **Introduction by Otto Penzler.**

John Dickson Carr, *The Plague Court Murders.* When murder occurs in a locked hut on Plague Court, an estate haunted by the ghost of a hangman's assistant who died a victim of the black death, Sir Henry Merrivale seeks a logical solution to a ghostly crime. A spiritual medium employed to rid the house of his spirit is found stabbed to death in a locked stone hut on the grounds, surrounded by an untouched circle of mud. **Introduction by Michael Dirda.**

John Dickson Carr, *The Red Widow Murders*. In a "haunted" mansion, the room known as the Red Widow's Chamber proves lethal to all who spend the night. Eight people investigate and the one who draws the ace of spades must sleep in it. The room is locked from the inside and watched all night by the others. When the door is unlocked, the victim has been poisoned. Enter Sir Henry Merrivale to solve the crime. **Introduction by Tom Mead.**

Frances Crane, *The Turquoise Shop*. In an arty little New Mexico town, Mona Brandon has arrived from the East and becomes the subject of gossip about her money, her influence, and the corpse in the nearby desert who may be her husband. Pat Holly, who runs the local gift shop, is as interested as anyone in the goings on—but even more in Pat Abbott, the detective investigating the possible murder. **Introduction by Anne Hillerman.**

Todd Downing, *Vultures in the Sky*. There is no end to the series of terrifying events that befall a luxury train bound for Mexico. First, a man dies when the train passes through a dark tunnel, then it comes to an abrupt stop in the middle of the desert. More deaths occur when night falls and the passengers panic when they realize they are trapped with a murderer on the loose. **Introduction by James Sallis.**

Mignon G. Eberhart, *Murder by an Aristocrat*. Nurse Keate is called to help a man who has been "accidentally" shot in the shoulder. When he is murdered while convalescing, it is clear that there was no accident. Although a killer is loose in the mansion, the family seems more concerned that news of the murder will leave their circle. *The New Yorker* wrote than "Eberhart can weave an almost flawless mystery." **Introduction by Nancy Pickard.**

Erle Stanley Gardner, *The Case of the Baited Hook*. Perry Mason gets a phone call in the middle of the night and his potential client says it's urgent, that he has two one-thousand-dollar bills that he will give him as a retainer, with an additional ten-thousand whenever he is called on to represent him. When

Mason takes the case, it is not for the caller but for a beautiful woman whose identity is hidden behind a mask. **Introduction by Otto Penzler.**

Erle Stanley Gardner, *The Case of the Borrowed Brunette*. A mysterious man named Mr. Hines has advertised a job for a woman who has to fulfill very specific physical requirements. Eva Martell, pretty but struggling in her career as a model, takes the job but her aunt smells a rat and hires Perry Mason to investigate. Her fears are realized when Hines turns up in the apartment with a bullet hole in his head. **Introduction by Otto Penzler.**

Erle Stanley Gardner, *The Case of the Careless Kitten*. Helen Kendal receives a mysterious phone call from her vanished uncle Franklin, long presumed dead, who urges her to contact Perry Mason. Soon, she finds herself the main suspect in the murder of an unfamiliar man. Her kitten has just survived a poisoning attempt—as has her aunt Matilda. What is the connection between Franklin's return and the murder attempts? **Introduction by Otto Penzler.**

Erle Stanley Gardner, *The Case of the Rolling Bones*. One of Gardner's most successful Perry Mason novels opens with a clear case of blackmail, though the person being blackmailed claims he isn't. It is not long before the police are searching for someone wanted for killing the same man in two different states—thirty-three years apart. The confounding puzzle of what happened to the dead man's toes is a challenge. **Introduction by Otto Penzler.**

Erle Stanley Gardner, *The Case of the Shoplifter's Shoe*. Most cases for Perry Mason involve murder but here he is hired because a young woman fears her aunt is a kleptomaniac. Sarah may not have been precisely the best guardian for a collection of valuable diamonds and, sure enough, they go missing. When the jeweler is found shot dead, Sarah is spotted leaving the murder scene with a bundle of gems stuffed in her purse. **Introduction by Otto Penzler.**

Erle Stanley Gardner, *The Bigger They Come*. Gardner's first novel using the pseudonym A.A. Fair starts off a series featuring the large and loud Bertha Cool and her employee, the small and meek Donald Lam. Given the job of delivering divorce papers to an evident crook,

Lam can't find him—but neither can the police. The *Los Angeles Times* called this book: "Breathlessly dramatic . . . an original." **Introduction by Otto Penzler.**

Frances Noyes Hart, *The Bellamy Trial.* Inspired by the real-life Hall-Mills case, the most sensational trial of its day, this is the story of Stephen Bellamy and Susan Ives, accused of murdering Bellamy's wife Madeleine. Eight days of dynamic testimony, some true, some not, make headlines for an enthralled public. Rex Stout called this historic courtroom thriller one of the ten best mysteries of all time. **Introduction by Hank Phillippi Ryan.**

H.F. Heard, *A Taste for Honey.* The elderly Mr. Mycroft quietly keeps bees in Sussex, where he is approached by the reclusive and somewhat misanthropic Mr. Silchester, whose honey supplier was found dead, stung to death by her bees. Mycroft, who shares many traits with Sherlock Holmes, sets out to find the vicious killer. Rex Stout described it as "sinister . . . a tale well and truly told." **Introduction by Otto Penzler.**

Dolores Hitchens, *The Alarm of the Black Cat.* Detective fiction aficionado Rachel Murdock has a peculiar meeting with a little girl and a dead toad, sparking her curiosity about a love triangle that has sparked anger. When the girl's great grandmother is found dead, Rachel and her cat Samantha work with a friend in the Los Angeles Police Department to get to the bottom of things. **Introduction by David Handler.**

Dolores Hitchens, *The Cat Saw Murder.* Miss Rachel Murdock, the highly intelligent 70-year-old amateur sleuth, is not entirely heartbroken when her slovenly, unattractive, bridge-cheating niece is murdered. Miss Rachel is happy to help the socially maladroit and somewhat bumbling Detective Lieutenant Stephen Mayhew, retaining her composure when a second brutal murder occurs. **Introduction by Joyce Carol Oates.**

Dorothy B. Hughes, *Dread Journey.* A bigshot Hollywood producer has worked on his magnum opus for years, hiring and firing one beautiful starlet after another. But Kitten Agnew's contract won't allow her to be fired, so she fears she might be terminated more permanently. Together with the producer on a train journey from Hollywood to Chicago, Kitten becomes more terrified with each passing mile. **Introduction by Sarah Weinman.**

Dorothy B. Hughes, *Ride the Pink Horse.* When Sailor met Willis Douglass, he was just a poor kid who Douglass groomed to work as a confidential secretary. As the senator became increasingly corrupt, he knew he could count on Sailor to clean up his messes. No longer a senator, Douglass flees Chicago for Santa Fe, leaving behind a murder rap and Sailor as the prime suspect. Seeking vengeance, Sailor follows. **Introduction by Sara Paretsky.**

Dorothy B. Hughes, *The So Blue Marble.* Set in the glamorous world of New York high society, this novel became a suspense classic as twins from Europe try to steal a rare and beautiful gem owned by an aristocrat whose sister is an even more menacing presence. *The New Yorker* called it "Extraordinary . . . [Hughes'] brilliant descriptive powers make and unmake reality." **Introduction by Otto Penzler.**

W. Bolingbroke Johnson, *The Widening Stain.* After a cocktail party, the attractive Lucie Coindreau, a "black-eyed, black-haired Frenchwoman" visits the rare books wing of the library and apparently takes a headfirst fall from an upper gallery. Dismissed as a horrible accident, it seems dubious when Professor Hyett is strangled while reading a priceless 12th-century manuscript, which has gone missing. **Introduction by Nicholas A. Basbanes**

Baynard Kendrick, *Blind Man's Bluff.* Blinded in World War II, Duncan Maclain forms a successful private detective agency, aided by his two dogs. Here, he is called on to solve the case of a blind man who plummets from the top of an eight-story building, apparently with no one present except his dead-drunk son. **Introduction by Otto Penzler.**

Baynard Kendrick, *The Odor of Violets.* Duncan Maclain, a blind former intelligence officer, is asked to investigate the murder of an actor in his Greenwich Village apartment. This would cause a stir at any time but, when the actor possesses secret government plans that then go missing, it's enough to interest the local police as well as the American government and Maclain, who suspects a German spy plot. **Introduction by Otto Penzler.**

C. Daly King, *Obelists at Sea*. On a cruise ship traveling from New York to Paris, the lights of the smoking room briefly go out, a gunshot crashes through the night, and a man is dead. Two detectives are on board but so are four psychiatrists who believe their professional knowledge can solve the case by understanding the psyche of the killer—each with a different theory. **Introduction by Martin Edwards.**

Jonathan Latimer, *Headed for a Hearse*. Featuring Bill Crane, the booze-soaked Chicago private detective, this humorous hard-boiled novel was filmed as *The Westland Case* in 1937 starring Preston Foster. Robert Westland has been framed for the grisly murder of his wife in a room with doors and windows locked from the inside. As the day of his execution nears, he relies on Crane to find the real murderer. **Introduction by Max Allan Collins**

Lange Lewis, *The Birthday Murder*. Victoria is a successful novelist and screenwriter and her husband is a movie director so their marriage seems almost too good to be true. Then, on her birthday, her happy new life comes crashing down when her husband is murdered using a method of poisoning that was described in one of her books. She quickly becomes the leading suspect. **Introduction by Randal S. Brandt.**

Frances and Richard Lockridge, *Death on the Aisle*. In one of the most beloved books to feature Mr. and Mrs. North, the body of a wealthy backer of a play is found dead in a seat of the 45th Street Theater. Pam is thrilled to engage in her favorite pastime—playing amateur sleuth—much to the annoyance of Jerry, her publisher husband. The Norths inspired a stage play, a film, and long-running radio and TV series. **Introduction by Otto Penzler.**

John P. Marquand, *Your Turn, Mr. Moto*. The first novel about Mr. Moto, originally titled *No Hero*, is the story of a World War I hero pilot who finds himself jobless during the Depression. In Tokyo for a big opportunity that falls apart, he meets a Japanese agent and his Russian colleague and the pilot suddenly finds himself caught in a web of intrigue. Peter Lorre played Mr. Moto in a series of popular films. **Introduction by Lawrence Block.**

Stuart Palmer, *The Penguin Pool Murder*. The first adventure of schoolteacher and dedicated amateur sleuth Hildegarde Withers occurs at the New York Aquarium when she and her young students notice a corpse in one of the tanks. It was published in 1931 and filmed the next year, starring Edna May Oliver as the American Miss Marple—though much funnier than her English counterpart. **Introduction by Otto Penzler.**

Stuart Palmer, *The Puzzle of the Happy Hooligan*. New York City schoolteacher Hildegarde Withers cannot resist "assisting" homicide detective Oliver Piper. In this novel, she is on vacation in Hollywood and on the set of a movie about Lizzie Borden when the screenwriter is found dead. Six comic films about Withers appeared in the 1930s, most successfully starring Edna May Oliver. **Introduction by Otto Penzler.**

Otto Penzler, ed., *Golden Age Bibliomysteries*. Stories of murder, theft, and suspense occur with alarming regularity in the unlikely world of books and bibliophiles, including bookshops, libraries, and private rare book collections, written by such giants of the mystery genre as Ellery Queen, Cornell Woolrich, Lawrence G. Blochman, Vincent Starrett, and Anthony Boucher. **Introduction by Otto Penzler.**

Otto Penzler, ed., *Golden Age Detective Stories*. The history of American mystery fiction has its pantheon of authors who have influenced and entertained readers for nearly a century, reaching its peak during the Golden Age, and this collection pays homage to the work of the most acclaimed: Cornell Woolrich, Erle Stanley Gardner, Craig Rice, Ellery Queen, Dorothy B. Hughes, Mary Roberts Rinehart, and more. **Introduction by Otto Penzler.**

Otto Penzler, ed., *Golden Age Locked Room Mysteries*. The so-called impossible crime category reached its zenith during the 1920s, 1930s, and 1940s, and this volume includes the greatest of the great authors who mastered the form: John Dickson Carr, Ellery Queen, C. Daly King, Clayton Rawson, and Erle Stanley Gardner. Like great magicians, these literary conjurors will baffle and delight readers. **Introduction by Otto Penzler.**

Ellery Queen, *The Adventures of Ellery Queen*. These stories are the earliest short works to feature Queen as a detective and are among the best of the author's fair-play mysteries. So many of the elements that comprise the gestalt of Queen may be found in these tales: alternate solutions, the dying clue, a bizarre crime, and the author's ability to find fresh variations of works by other authors. **Introduction by Otto Penzler.**

Ellery Queen, *The American Gun Mystery.* A rodeo comes to New York City at the Colosseum. The headliner is Buck Horne, the once popular film cowboy who opens the show leading a charge of forty whooping cowboys until they pull out their guns and fire into the air. Buck falls to the ground, shot dead. The police instantly lock the doors to search everyone but the offending weapon has completely vanished. **Introduction by Otto Penzler.**

Ellery Queen, *The Chinese Orange Mystery.* The offices of publisher Donald Kirk have seen strange events but nothing like this. A strange man is found dead with two long spears alongside his back. And, though no one was seen entering or leaving the room, everything has been turned backwards or upside down: pictures face the wall, the victim's clothes are worn backwards, the rug upside down. Why in the world? **Introduction by Otto Penzler.**

Ellery Queen, *The Dutch Shoe Mystery.* Millionaire philanthropist Abagail Doorn falls into a coma and she is rushed to the hospital she funds for an emergency operation by one of the leading surgeons on the East Coast. When she is wheeled into the operating theater, the sheet covering her body is pulled back to reveal her garroted corpse—the first of a series of murders **Introduction by Otto Penzler.**

Ellery Queen, *The Egyptian Cross Mystery.* A small-town schoolteacher is found dead, headed, and tied to a T-shaped cross on December 25th, inspiring such sensational headlines as "Crucifixion on Christmas Day." Amateur sleuth Ellery Queen is so intrigued he travels to Virginia but fails to solve the crime. Then a similar murder takes place on New York's Long Island—and then another. **Introduction by Otto Penzler.**

Ellery Queen, *The Siamese Twin Mystery.* When Ellery and his father encounter a raging forest fire on a mountain, their only hope is to drive up to an isolated hillside manor owned by a secretive surgeon and his strange guests. While playing solitaire in the middle of the night, the doctor is shot. The only clue is a torn playing card. Suspects include a society beauty, a valet, and conjoined twins. **Introduction by Otto Penzler.**

Ellery Queen, *The Spanish Cape Mystery.* Amateur detective Ellery Queen arrives in the resort town of Spanish Cape soon after a young woman and her uncle are abducted by a gun-toting, one-eyed giant. The next day, the woman's somewhat dicey boyfriend is found murdered—totally naked under a black fedora and opera cloak. **Introduction by Otto Penzler.**

Patrick Quentin, *A Puzzle for Fools.* Broadway producer Peter Duluth takes to the bottle when his wife dies but enters a sanitarium to dry out. Malevolent events plague the hospital, including when Peter hears his own voice intone, "There will be murder." And there is. He investigates, aided by a young woman who is also a patient. This is the first of nine mysteries featuring Peter and Iris Duluth. **Introduction by Otto Penzler.**

Clayton Rawson, *Death from a Top Hat.* When the New York City Police Department is baffled by an apparently impossible crime, they call on The Great Merlini, a retired stage magician who now runs a Times Square magic shop. In his first case, two occultists have been murdered in a room locked from the inside, their bodies positioned to form a pentagram. **Introduction by Otto Penzler.**

Craig Rice, *Eight Faces at Three.* Gin-soaked John J. Malone, defender of the guilty, is notorious for getting his culpable clients off. It's the innocent ones who are problems. Like Holly Inglehart, accused of piercing the black heart of her well-heeled aunt Alexandria with a lovely Florentine paper cutter. No one who knew the old battle-ax liked her, but Holly's prints were found on the murder weapon. **Introduction by Lisa Lutz.**

Craig Rice, *Home Sweet Homicide.* Known as the Dorothy Parker of mystery fiction for her memorable wit, Craig Rice was the first detective writer to appear on the cover of *Time* magazine. This comic mystery features two kids who are trying to find a husband for their widowed mother while she's engaged in sleuthing. Filmed with the same title in 1946 with Peggy Ann Garner and Randolph Scott. **Introduction by Otto Penzler.**

Mary Roberts Rinehart, *The Album*. Crescent Place is a quiet enclave of wealthy people in which nothing ever happens—until a bedridden old woman is attacked by an intruder with an ax. *The New York Times* stated: "All Mary Roberts Rinehart mystery stories are good, but this one is better." **Introduction by Otto Penzler.**

Mary Roberts Rinehart, *The Haunted Lady*. The arsenic in her sugar bowl was wealthy widow Eliza Fairbanks' first clue that somebody wanted her dead. Nightly visits of bats, birds, and rats, obviously aimed at scaring the dowager to death, was the second. Eliza calls the police, who send nurse Hilda Adams, the amateur sleuth they refer to as "Miss Pinkerton," to work undercover to discover the culprit. **Introduction by Otto Penzler.**

Mary Roberts Rinehart, *Miss Pinkerton*. Hilda Adams is a nurse, not a detective, but she is observant and smart and so it is common for Inspector Patton to call on her for help. Her success results in his calling her "Miss Pinkerton." *The New Republic* wrote: "From thousands of hearts and homes the cry will go up: Thank God for Mary Roberts Rinehart." **Introduction by Carolyn Hart.**

Mary Roberts Rinehart, *The Red Lamp*. Professor William Porter refuses to believe that the seaside manor he's just inherited is haunted but he has to convince his wife to move in. However, he soon sees evidence of the occult phenomena of which the townspeople speak. Whether it is a spirit or a human being, Porter accepts that there is a connection to the rash of murders that have terrorized the countryside. **Introduction by Otto Penzler.**

Mary Roberts Rinehart, *The Wall*. For two decades, Mary Roberts Rinehart was the second-best-selling author in America (only Sinclair Lewis outsold her) and was beloved for her tales of suspense. In a magnificent mansion, the ex-wife of one of the owners turns up making demands and is found dead the next day. And there are more dark secrets lying behind the walls of the estate. **Introduction by Otto Penzler.**

Joel Townsley Rogers, *The Red Right Hand*. This extraordinary whodunnit that is as puzzling as it is terrifying was identified by crime fiction scholar Jack Adrian as "one of the dozen or so finest mystery novels of the 20th century." A deranged killer sends a doctor on a quest for the truth—deep into the recesses of his own mind—when he and his bride-to-be elope but pick up a terrifying sharp-toothed hitch-hiker. **Introduction by Joe R. Lansdale.**

Roger Scarlett, *Cat's Paw*. The family of the wealthy old bachelor Martin Greenough cares far more about his money than they do about him. For his birthday, he invites all his potential heirs to his mansion to tell them what they hope to hear. Before he can disburse funds, however, he is murdered, and the Boston Police Department's big problem is that there are too many suspects. **Introduction by Curtis Evans**

Vincent Starrett, *Dead Man Inside*. 1930s Chicago is a tough town but some crimes are more bizarre than others. Customers arrive at a haberdasher to find a corpse in the window and a sign on the door: *Dead Man Inside! I am Dead. The store will not open today.* This is just one of a series of odd murders that terrorizes the city. Reluctant detective Walter Ghost leaps into action to learn what is behind the plague. **Introduction by Otto Penzler.**

Vincent Starrett, *The Great Hotel Murder*. Theater critic and amateur sleuth Riley Blackwood investigates a murder in a Chicago hotel where the dead man had changed rooms with a stranger who had registered under a fake name. *The New York Times* described it as "an ingenious plot with enough complications to keep the reader guessing." **Introduction by Lyndsay Faye.**

Vincent Starrett, *Murder on 'B' Deck*. Walter Ghost, a psychologist, scientist, explorer, and former intelligence officer, is on a cruise ship and his friend novelist Dunsten Mollock, a Nigel Bruce-like Watson whose role is to offer occasional comic relief, accommodates when he fails to leave the ship before it takes off. Although they make mistakes along the way, the amateur sleuths solve the shipboard murders. **Introduction by Ray Betzner.**

Phoebe Atwood Taylor, *The Cape Cod Mystery*. Vacationers have flocked to Cape Cod to avoid the heat wave that hit the Northeast and find their holiday unpleasant when the area is flooded with police trying to find the murderer of a muckraking journalist who took a cottage for the season. Finding a solution falls to Asey Mayo, "the Cape Cod Sherlock," known for his worldly wisdom, folksy humor, and common sense. **Introduction by Otto Penzler.**

S. S. Van Dine, *The Benson Murder Case.* The first of 12 novels to feature Philo Vance, the most popular and influential detective character of the early part of the 20th century. When wealthy stockbroker Alvin Benson is found shot to death in a locked room in his mansion, the police are baffled until the erudite flaneur and art collector arrives on the scene. Paramount filmed it in 1930 with William Powell as Vance. **Introduction by Ragnar Jónasson.**

Cornell Woolrich, *The Bride Wore Black.* The first suspense novel by one of the greatest of all noir authors opens with a bride and her new husband walking out of the church. A car speeds by, shots ring out, and he falls dead at her feet. Determined to avenge his death, she tracks down everyone in the car, concluding with a shocking surprise. It was filmed by Francois Truffaut in 1968, starring Jeanne Moreau. **Introduction by Eddie Muller.**

Cornell Woolrich, *Deadline at Dawn.* Quinn is overcome with guilt about having robbed a stranger's home. He meets Bricky, a dime-a-dance girl, and they fall for each other. When they return to the crime scene, they discover a dead body. Knowing Quinn will be accused of the crime, they race to find the true killer before he's arrested. A 1946 film starring Susan Hayward was loosely based on the plot. **Introduction by David Gordon.**

Cornell Woolrich, *Waltz into Darkness.* A New Orleans businessman successfully courts a woman through the mail but he is shocked to find when she arrives that she is not the plain brunette whose picture he'd received but a radiant blond beauty. She soon absconds with his fortune. Wracked with disappointment and loneliness, he vows to track her down. When he finds her, the real nightmare begins. **Introduction by Wallace Stroby.**